The Secret of Telfair Inn

The Secret of Telfair Inn

REVISED EDITION

Idella Bodie
Idella Bodie

with illustrations
by Louise Yancey

SANDLAPPER PUBLISHING CO., INC.

THE SECRET OF TELFAIR INN
Copyright © 1995 Idella Bodie
Copyright © 1971 Sandlapper Publishing Co., Inc.

First printing, 1971, hardcover
Second printing, 1983, softcover
Third printing, 1986
Fourth printing, 2001 — Revised Edition

ISBN 0-87844-050-X

Published by Sandlapper Publishing Co., Inc.
Orangeburg, SC 29115

Manufactured in the United States of America

Library of Congress Cataloging-in-Publication Data

Bodie, Idella.
    The secret of Telfair Inn. Illus. by Louise Yancey.   [1st ed. Columbia,
S.C.] Sandlapper Press [1971]
        98 p.   illus.   23 cm.
    Summary: While staying in an old South Carolina inn, two children
become intrigued by the mystery connected with the unusued portion of
the building.
        ISBN 0-87844-007-0

    [1. Mystery and detective stories]   I. Yancey, Louise, illus.   II.Title
PZ7.B63525 Se   [Fic]   79-1779909
                                                                  MARC
    Library of Congress   86[r87]rev2   AC

To Beth and John,
who were always curious about old houses

Although there is an old inn in Aiken that kindled the spark for this story, the facts included here are purely fictional, as are the characters. The historical facts and places are true, having been researched and documented in the Aiken County Public Library and the Minnie B. Kennedy Junior High School Library.

Idella Bodie

Contents

1. Going South / 1
2. Silas Crowe / 8
3. Getting Acquainted / 15
4. Shadows in the Dark / 22
5. A Mysterious Happening / 28
6. Making Friends / 37
7. Trespassing / 48
8. Wild Goose Chase / 58
9. A Time to Dream / 68
10. The Secret of the Inn / 78
11. Coker Spring / 93
12. A Terrible Accident / 102
13. A Visit to the Hospital / 111
14. Happy Ending / 117

The Secret of
Telfair Inn

1.
Going South

"Hey, Dad," Marcy called from the back seat of the Dunlaps' station wagon, "that sign said 'Aiken—2 miles.'"

"It's about time," Marcy's older brother Phil griped.

Weeks earlier Mr. Dunlap announced to his family that the northern university where he taught wanted him to go to South Carolina for historical research. Marcy and Phil had not liked the idea at all. They loved the short trips they'd made with their dad before, but *the whole summer!* That was something else.

"Gee, Dad," Phil had complained, "that'll mean the relay team'll have a missing link."

"Now, Philip," Mrs. Dunlap said, "your dad's so pleased to be asked to do this for the university. It's quite an honor. We don't want to spoil it for him, do we?"

Watching her brother's brow furrow, Marcy guessed what he was thinking. Last summer he helped set track team records. He would miss challenging the other boys.

Marcy was always good for an idea, and as usual she had one. "I know — Phil could stay with Aunt Grace." As soon as the words left her mouth she was sorry. Who would she hang out with if Phil stayed behind? If no one else was around, her older brother let her tag along.

In an attempt to take back her suggestion, she said, "At least Phil doesn't have a best friend to leave behind the way I do. Ellen and I have been best friends since third grade, and in August we'll have our birthdays, and I won't be here." She pursed her lips, forcing the freckles along her nose to run together.

In spite of a ruined summer, Marcy had found it exciting when their dad got out the road map to trace their journey south. Like her brother, the chance for adventure always put a twinkle in her kitten-gray eyes. Time seemed to rush to the date set for departure.

The Dunlaps were riding for the second long day to reach their destination. As the road unfolded before them, Marcy grew fidgety with the anticipation of seeing their summer home.

She and Phil jumped at every opportunity to climb from their seats between their dad's books and their mom's fresh linens and stretch their legs.

"Oh, look!" Mrs. Dunlap exclaimed as they entered the town of Aiken. "Magnolias — and in bloom too. Those creamy-white blossoms make gorgeous arrangements. But you can't touch them or they'll yellow."

Tom Dunlap smiled at his wife, and Marcy knew he must be thinking what a flower lover she was. "Aiken is known for its magnificent trees and gardens," he said. "It's a small resort town." Mr. Dunlap had told his family very little about the place they would visit, but he said the furnished apartment building they were to live in was a fashionable inn years before.

"Scores of famous people have lived in Aiken," he continued. "Many of the old mansions were left to schools and churches. Of course some wealthy homeowners still come for the winter months."

"That's funny," Phil said. "They go north for the summer and we come south." A groan trailed his words, reminding the others he had not forgotten what he left behind. But his mood improved abruptly as he noticed the name of the

3

highway they turned onto. "Whiskey Road!" he read.

"What an intriguing name," Mrs. Dunlap said. "There must be a story behind that, Tom. . . . Oh, look at that lovely serpentine wall with the ivy trailing over it."

"There's a gate in it," Marcy announced.

Mr. Dunlap slowed the car, as they all took in the scenery. The streets were wide and there was little traffic. Late afternoon sunlight streamed through the giant magnolias, splattering the pavement. Hanging oak tree branches formed an arch over their car. Azalea bushes flanked the roadside.

"It's such a lovely town!" Mrs. Dunlap sighed, smiling. "Wish the azaleas were in bloom."

"Let's see," Mr. Dunlap mused as he approached a traffic light. "The realtor's letter said, a left here, then follow the road to the wooden bridge. The apartment building is called Telfair Inn." He turned onto another shady road that wound down a steep hill.

Mrs. Dunlap pointed left. "Those look like stables."

"Aiken is famous for horses," Mr. Dunlap explained, concentrating too hard on following the realtor's directions for conversation.

They continued down the shady lane under the tree canopy, noting stables and woods on either side.

Marcy imagined a colony of gnomes as they drove through a forest of ancient magnolias. Giant gnarled limbs created an impassable maze. Wound around low-hanging branches, vines twisted and turned right up to the edge of the road.

"It must be just ahead," Mr. Dunlap said as they started up another hill. "Yes, this is it. The realtor said construction was going on across the street."

"And there's the wooden bridge." Mrs. Dunlap smoothed her soft chestnut-colored hair.

From the back seat Marcy strained to see. The car broke from the shade, and she couldn't believe her eyes. A mansion stood before them. Tall columns supported the front porch that stretched the width of the building. Sunlight reflected off the fresh coat of white paint. But much of the back part of the rambling old inn lay in ruin.

Beside her, Phil leaned low to get a better view of the irregular roof line of the gabled house and the aged chimneys jutting skyward.

"Wow! Look at those lightning rods!" he shouted.

In spite of the inn's enormous size, the yard was small. Mr. Dunlap parked the car just over the wooden bridge, near the front entrance.

Phil sprang from the car and ran through bamboo that thinly hedged a gigantic ravine. In seconds Marcy was behind him.

Standing at the edge, Marcy shrieked, "Geez!" From the bottom of the gorge a tiny voice echoed, "Geez!"

"Philip! Marcia! Come with us," Mrs. Dunlap called, climbing the steps to the veranda.

Marcy and Phil pulled themselves away from the ravine, but not before they caught sight of the vines hanging like ropes down the sides. They followed their parents into the entrance hall.

"Dad," Marcy said, pulling at her father's sleeve, "you gotta see—"

"Just a minute, Marcy—one thing at a time. Let's find out who's in charge here."

The Dunlaps stood in the dim hallway straining to see. The only light came through the screened door they had just entered. Late afternoon shadows fell across deep wine carpet, giving a crimson tint to the still air. The eery feel was reflected in a tall mirror hanging above the massive carved chest. The high ceiling seemed miles above the five dark doors opening off the great hallway.

Marcy felt a shiver down her spine and she edged closer to her father.

2.
Silas Crowe

From somewhere behind a wall there was a creaking of boards as if someone was walking up stairs. A key clicked in a lock at the far end of the long hallway. A doorknob turned. The Dunlaps waited in silence as the door swung open.

An elderly, stoop-shouldered man, clad in overalls, hobbled toward them. He peered through thick glasses that magnified his deep-set eyes.

"Yeah? What is it?" The stranger's voice seemed to come from an endless cavern. Years had scarred the old man's face with sharp lines, and rheumatism gnarled and twisted his body. He flailed his cane in the air.

Marcy watched, petrified, as her father extended his hand. "I'm Tom Dunlap and this is my family. We're the new tenants."

The man scowled at Marcy and Phil. His thin lips formed a straight line, like another crease in his wrinkled face. "Ain't s'posed to be no younguns."

Marcy's dad was tall and thin. His close clipped hair made him look even taller. Mr. Dunlap looked down at the man in his usual relaxed and easy-going manner, but when he spoke, Marcy could tell he was annoyed. "They're not children. They're very grown-up. They won't disturb anyone."

Phil stood tall. Marcy knew her brother resented being called a "youngun." And, since he'd seen the ravine, she knew he was thinking they just had to stay here!

Marcy looked from her dad to Phil, then to her mom, and back to the scowling old man. She tried to put on her sweetest angelic expression.

The man growled, "Nobody but grownups allowed in these apartments." With a crippled hand he pushed his heavy glasses up on his bulbous nose.

"But didn't the realtor tell you?" Mr. Dunlap went on. "He knew about Marcy and Phil. I've already signed a lease for the summer."

"I keep telling them this ain't no place for

younguns," the old man persisted. His scowl, the peering eyes, the large nose — all topped by wild white hair — frightened Marcy.

At last Mrs. Dunlap spoke. "Oh, if you mean because of the ravine, don't worry. They won't get hurt. They're very responsible."

Growing impatient, Mr. Dunlap sighed heavily. "We've had a long trip down from New York," he said. "We're tired and eager to get settled. If you'll just show us — "

"There's *no trespassing* signs all over this place," the old man interrupted. Marcy figured he was referring to the old part of the inn she noticed when they drove up. The stranger stood without moving, except to lift his cane and let it bang the floor now and then.

"All right, Mr. — " Mr. Dunlap began, the sound of defeat in his voice.

"Crowe." The old man spat his name. "Silas Crowe."

"All right, Mr. Crowe, at least let us stay overnight. I'll speak to Mr. Beard at the realtor's office in the morning and get this straightened out."

The old man hesitated, then lifted a grimy string attached to his belt. He rattled keys until he'd singled out a certain one. Shuffling, as if his bowed legs were stiff, he moved to one of the massive doors on the left and, with another rattling of keys, unlocked it.

Mrs. Dunlap caught her breath when the door was opened. "Why, it's beautiful!" she said. The sitting room was elaborately decorated. Heavy drapes hung at the windows. Overstuffed chairs were arranged around a marble fireplace. Above the mantel was a great mirror much like the one in the hall. Elegant furniture stood against papered walls.

Before Mrs. Dunlap could move to the kitchen, Silas Crowe was hobbling toward a spiral staircase. "This goes up to your bedroom and bathroom. More stairs take you to a second bedroom and bath." Again he frowned at the children and ran a hand across his mop of hair.

"You mean this is a three-story apartment?" Mr. Dunlap asked.

"That's right. They cut it up that way when they remodeled." His words came out as if he resented having to speak at all.

"If you want me," he mumbled, "knock loud on that door I came out of."

"Thank you," replied Mr. Dunlap, upset over the turn things had taken.

The old man shuffled toward the door, muttering "No place for younguns" under his breath.

The moment Mr. Crowe's back was turned Phil dashed up the stairs that circled to the first bedroom. Marcy took off after him.

"Oh, man!" Marcy heard Phil shout from somewhere above her.

Following his voice, she climbed more spiral stairs to a spacious bedroom, its ceiling slanted on one side. "This is our room!" she squealed.

"You mean if that eccentric old man lets us stay," Phil answered, crossing to a window. "Say, we've got a good view of the ravine from here."

Marcy's attention had been captured by an antique pitcher and washbasin fitted into a stand made especially for them. The oval mirror above the stand looked like one she had seen in a movie about the Old West. The twin beds had brass bedposts. One bed was beside a window that lead to a fire escape.

Mrs. Dunlap's voice drifted up as if from the bottom of a barrel. "Philip! Marcy! Come down and help bring in our bags."

Marcy raced her brother down the two flights of spiral stairs. This might not be such a dull summer after all! she thought.

3.
Getting Acquainted

Now that Mr. Crowe was out of sight and the luggage was in, Marcy and Phil couldn't wait to explore. They dashed outside the minute Mrs. Dunlap gave the go-ahead.

Running toward the bamboo hedge, Marcy asked, "Are you going down in it?"

Just a few feet beyond the hedge, the land fell away into a deep gorge stretching left and right as far as they could see. Phil stood studying the ravine. "That railroad track at the bottom isn't used anymore. Weeds have grown over the rails."

It made Marcy dizzy to look over the edge where small trees and vines hugged the cliff.

"Are you going down?" she repeated.

Phil was lost in thought and didn't answer.

14

Instead, he turned and walked toward the bridge.

That would be the best place to climb down, Marcy thought. We could hold on to the supports beneath the bridge.

Marcy and Phil were running along the edge of the ravine when Mr. Dunlap came outside. Joining them, he marveled at the Tarzan-sized wisteria vines winding around the tall pines, oaks, dogwoods, and Carolina cherry trees.

"Ah," he sighed as he stretched his arms wide and took a deep breath. "Smell that sweet honeysuckle."

"Where's the honeysuckle?" asked Marcy, not wanting to miss a thing.

"Everywhere," Mr. Dunlap answered. "See — there . . . and there — the vine with the funnel-shaped yellow blooms."

The three walked onto the old wooden bridge crossing the ravine. From the middle they had a good view of the front and one side of the inn. The front had been freshly painted and renovated, but the sprawling side suffered from neglect. Many seasons had eaten into the wood, warping the boards and peeling the paint. Panes were broken in some of the windows, and shutters hung loose. Large-leafed vines ran everywhere, even covering some of the windows. The old inn looked like a haunted house.

"This place has more gables than Nathaniel Hawthorne's *House of Seven Gables!*" exclaimed Phil.

Not wanting to admit she hadn't read the book, Marcy counted. "Yeah, it's got nine," she said. At least she knew what a gable was.

Across the bridge the road opened onto a boulevard bordered by a thick forest. The varying shades of green made it seem almost as colorful as the woods back home in autumn. Mr. Dunlap pointed out the honeysuckle growing at the base of the trees and onto the branches.

Pointing to a vine with yellow flowers, he said, "This is jessamine, South Carolina's state flower. The tiny yellow trumpets give it the sweet smell, but they're deadly poisonous."

Something stirring in the underbrush caught their attention. A squirrel sat up, watched them for a moment with his shoe-button eyes, then scampered up a nearby pine. They all laughed.

Following the winding street, they came to a small brick building with a heavy oak door.

"What do you know!" Mr. Dunlap exclaimed. "The library! How lucky can a man be."

"But if nasty old Mr. Crowe makes us leave," said Phil, "you may not be near the library after all."

"Don't worry about that, Son. I'm sure Mr. Beard will take care of it in the morning."

Marcy wasn't worried. She believed her daddy could fix just about anything.

A Presbyterian church stood next to the library. From there they had a view of Aiken's main street. There was little activity at this hour — an occasional car passing — since all the shops and offices were already closed. It was so different from New York!

Crossing the wide street, they admired a fountain encircled by spreading juniper and clumps of orange, red, and yellow day lilies.

Marcy smiled. "Mom'll like that."

The imposing post office, with its steep steps and shiny brass rails, stood catercornered on the other side of the street.

Woods, mostly pine trees stretching tall to get their share of sunlight, formed on the other side of the boulevard. Several dirt roads with signs reading "Private" in neat black letters led to hidden homes.

Walking back over the bridge they saw the

hulking machinery standing idle after a day's work on the new apartment building across from Telfair Inn. Silhouetted against the lemon-colored sunset, the machines looked like prehistoric monsters rising on the horizon.

"That bulldozer looks like a dinosaur," Phil said, laughing. The others agreed.

"Let's see if your mom wants to come outside for a few minutes before it gets dark," Mr. Dunlap said as they approached the inn.

About that time they noticed Mrs. Dunlap standing on the veranda, smiling and talking with a handsome young couple.

"Tom! Children!" she called. "Come meet the Fergusons, our neighbors across the hall."

After everyone said hello, Marcy looked at Phil. She could tell he was itching to get back to the ravine. But at that moment the mention of Mr. Crowe's name caught her attention. Marcy realized she was scared to death of that man.

"Mrs. Dunlap was just telling us of Mr. Crowe's greeting." Mr. Ferguson smiled.

"Oh, yes," nodded Mr. Dunlap.

"It seems," said Mrs. Ferguson, "that Mr. Crowe's parents were personal servants of the original owners of this inn. For some reason he acts as if he owns the place. I'm told he brought

Mrs. Crowe here to live after they were married, and many years later when the inn closed, she and Mr. Crowe stayed on as caretakers."

"Then he has a wife?" asked Mrs. Dunlap.

"Rumor has it she went to Philadelphia five or six years ago to live with relatives on her mother's side of the family," Mr. Ferguson responded.

"I wouldn't blame her," said Mrs. Ferguson, with a glance toward her husband.

"He's eccentric," Phil said.

"That's for sure," Mr. Ferguson agreed. "Why, in the spring he refused to allow a razing crew to tear down the dilapidated part of this building, after the new owners had given them instructions to begin the work."

"He went out with his cane and stopped them right in the act," Mrs. Ferguson added.

"And they let him?" asked Mr. Dunlap.

"He told them he had been given permission to live here the rest of his life," Mr. Ferguson said. "He lives in the old part, you know. Actually, I think they just pacified him by postponing the inevitable. The current owner definitely isn't going to renovate any more of this building with those new apartments coming up across the street. The old section will have to come down."

"It certainly is an eyesore," said Mr. Dunlap.

"That it is," agreed Mr. Ferguson.

Marcy didn't think it was an eyesore. She liked the way it looked.

As soon as the conversation switched to the Dunlaps' reason for coming south, Phil rounded the corner of the inn, with Marcy following close behind.

Standing next to the hedge bordering the inn side of the ravine, Phil studied the old building. "Look! That's our room—way up there."

"Which one?"

"The gabled window with the fire escape and the one to the right of it."

"I'm getting the bed by the fire escape," Marcy said. She looked at Phil thinking she'd get an argument.

But he turned and headed for the bridge. Marcy knew he was trying to determine the best way to get to the bottom of that ravine.

4.
Shadows in the Night

Marcy and Phil were called in for the night before they had a chance to get to the bottom of the ravine, but they had explored enough for Marcy to know it would be no easy task. Phil would find a way—she knew that.

As Marcy lay in her bed by the fire escape window, she thought of the fun she'd had already. She even enjoyed taking a bath in the old bathtub with claw feet.

"Phil?" Marcy called across to her brother's bed. "Why do you think Mr. Crowe doesn't want us here?"

"Because he's odd. Dad says we'll stay and we will."

Marcy turned on her stomach and bunched her pillow under her chin. "Phil, have you ever been down a fire escape?"

"Just think—I have to room with Miss Chatterbox for a whole summer!"

Ignoring her brother's remark, Marcy said, "But in case there's a fire, shouldn't we know how to go down the fire escape?"

"What do you suggest? A fire drill—now?"

"Of course, not now." Marcy peered around the bedpost and out the window into the night.

"Then keep quiet and go to sleep," Phil barked.

Marcy wasn't in the mood for sleep. Her mind was racing with thoughts about the old inn. She imagined all the famous people who must have slept here and all the fancy parties. She lay listening to the night sounds: the soft whistling of the wind, the faint tapping of a loose shutter, the chirping of crickets. Somewhere across the ravine a sweet-throated bird was singing. A sound she couldn't identify reminded her of the mew of a cat, then the whistle of a train. An occasional car crossed the wooden bridge.

Marcy always thought of this time of night as the "whisper time." How different it was here from the whisper time in New York. She looked up into the dark velvet sky. Summer stars twinkled at her. She felt a sudden chill. *Why doesn't Mr. Crowe want us here?* she wondered.

"Phil," she called in a low voice.

The steady breathing from the other bed told her Phil was fast asleep.

Marcy prided herself on not being a fraidy-cat—and she wasn't afraid now, she told herself. All of a sudden she remembered Herman, the stuffed frog she always carried with her for luck. He was still in her suitcase.

Slipping her feet to the floor, she crossed the room in the faint moonlight. She bent over and rummaged through the contents of her suitcase until she felt the familiar body. She hugged Herman to her neck and was just straightening up when she collided with someone.

Mrs. Dunlap gasped, "Oh, Marcy! You startled me."

"Me too," Marcy giggled.

"I just wanted to check on you," her mother whispered, realizing Phil was asleep. "You seem so far away up here."

"I'm okay. I'll knock on the floor and yell if I need you," Marcy whispered, as she gave a nervous laugh.

"All right." Mrs. Dunlap gave her daughter's shoulders a squeeze and tiptoed back downstairs.

Her mom's visit and Herman's closeness restored Marcy's confidence. Instead of getting back into bed, she stood by the open window. Pressing her nose against the screen, she could see down the far end of the ravine. The moonlight lay on the rails in long streaks of silver.

With a *snap*, the screen slipped from the window and fell to rest on the fire escape. Marcy jumped. Then, realizing what had happened, she eased herself onto the windowsill and strained to make out shapes in the darkness.

This is like the balcony in the movie theatre, she thought. Across the ravine she could see the outline of trees, black against the night sky. Fireflies, flickering on and off, played hide and seek at the edge of the woods. The moon hung suspended above the trees like a great bubble. A cloud crossed the sky, bursting the bubble for a moment.

Marcy's eyes burned from staring into the thick night and she squeezed them tight. When she opened them again and looked into the ravine, she caught her breath. Two figures moved at a snail's pace along the railroad track, going away from the inn. She could barely make them out, silhouetted against the night. One looked

like the hunched body of Mr. Crowe.

How had they gotten into the ravine? And why would they be walking the track at this time of night?

Suddenly the night air seemed cool. Shivering, Marcy climbed back in, reached through the window for the screen, and fit it back into place. She closed the window and locked it. Crawling into bed she pulled up the covers and hugged Herman tight.

She wished Phil were awake so she could tell him what she'd seen.

"Phil?" she whispered again. His rhythmic breathing was his only response.

5.
A Mysterious Happening

When Marcy woke the next morning, she could not remember where she was. Then the events of the previous day came rushing back. She sat up in bed and looked out the window. The day was clear and sunny. Envious that Phil was already up, she threw on her clothes. She quickly brushed her teeth, ran a comb through her long hair, and hurried downstairs.

Mr. Dunlap was in his usual good mood at breakfast and eager to get started on his research. "I'll dash by Mr. Beard's office and confirm our lease, then go on to the library," he said. "Will you meet me there later?"

"I'd love to," Mrs. Dunlap said. "I have very little unpacking left, but I do need to find a grocery store before lunch."

"Phil? Marcy?" Mr. Dunlap asked.

Marcy looked at Phil. She didn't want to go, and she knew wild horses couldn't drag Phil away this morning.

"Maybe this afternoon, Dad," Phil answered. "I'd like to look around here this morning."

"Me too," Marcy said.

"All right. I'll see you later then," Mr. Dunlap said.

"Be careful around the ravine," Mrs. Dunlap warned. "And by all means stay away from the construction across the street."

And Mr. Crowe, thought Marcy.

As Phil and Marcy helped clear the breakfast dishes, Mrs. Dunlap reminded them how grown up and responsible they were.

"If anything happens while we're away," she cautioned, "one of you run up to the library. Your dad tells me it's just across the bridge."

No sooner had their mother headed for the library than Marcy and Phil ran to the ravine. The noise from the construction site was loud, and they had to shout to hear each other.

They discovered that the bridge was not a good place to go down after all. The wooden supports were splintery, and it would be impossible to slide down wearing summer shorts. Phil spied a spot with less dense undergrowth. Marcy watched as he turned around, his back to the gorge, and started down.

"If these scrub oaks will hold me," he called up to her, "they'll hold you. Come on."

With a slight quickening in her stomach, Marcy turned around, grabbed the closest tree limb, and dropped her body over the edge. For a moment she was suspended, then her foot found a hold.

She inched down, feeling along the steep incline for one firm foothold after another. Once she slipped and lost her footing. Several times her hair caught in twigs. Afraid to turn loose to free it, she continued down, leaving strands of red behind.

"How much farther?" she called, not daring to look below.

"I'm almost there!" Phil shouted. Then a resounding *thump* told her he had reached the bottom.

If Phil could do it, she could. Half sliding and half climbing, she worked her way down the steep embankment. At last, hot and scratched, she stood on the ravine floor. There were red marks on her legs and arms, and her hands stung from holding on to the branches so tight. Perspiration ran in rivulets down her face.

Marcy pushed her hair back and looked up at the sky. "Whew!" she said. They were going to have to get back out of this place, she realized—but she wouldn't think about that now.

Phil was down on his hands and knees with his head to the rail. Marcy couldn't imagine why, but she did the same. The cold steel of the rail felt good to her stinging hands, but the strong smell of tar from the crossties made her nose itch.

"I read," said Phil, lifting his head, "that you can hear a train coming miles and miles away like that."

Marcy jumped up. "But you said this track wasn't used anymore." The idea of a train coming now was scary. Only a few feet of available space lay on either side of the track.

"It isn't. I was just telling you what I've read." Phil turned toward the bridge and started walking a rail, balancing himself by stretching his arms out from his sides.

Marcy copied him. "This is fun!" she called. Noise from the construction site was faint down in the gorge, and Marcy thought her voice had an odd, hollow sound.

Slipping and laughing and getting up again, they walked the rails side by side until they crossed under the bridge. As far as they could see, the great cut in the earth continued.

"We'd better turn around," Marcy said.

"I guess so," Phil agreed, "but there's no way we can get lost. All we'd have to do is just follow the track."

They turned and started back toward the inn, still tottering and giggling in their attempts to walk the rails without slipping onto the loose gravel between the crossties.

"Hey, see if you can do it with your eyes closed!" Phil called. He had mastered his first attempts to balance himself on the slender rail, and now he wanted more of a challenge.

They were almost under the bridge again when Marcy slipped. She opened her eyes and looked up. For a moment she stood stock-still, too frightened to move or call out. Mr. Crowe was coming down the railroad track toward them!

"Ph-Phil—"

"Huh?"

"Look!" She pointed to the hunched figure with his head down, picking his way along with his cane.

Phil darted behind the base of the bridge. "Come on," he called in a half whisper. "We can hide here until he passes."

"But he'll see us."

"Not if we hide behind these bushes."

"But—"

"But what?" Phil was getting impatient.

Marcy didn't want to admit it, but she remembered seeing lizards scurry around wooded areas. Not that she'd mind holding one, but she didn't want one slithering up her leg.

"Come on!" Phil urged.

Mustering courage, she squeezed into the space Phil provided. After all, a lizard was the lesser of the two evils.

They hid behind the great wooden beam for what seemed forever to Marcy before Phil whispered, "I'm going to peek out."

Braced against the side of the ravine in fear, Marcy watched as the look on her brother's face changed to one of puzzlement.

"Where'd he go?" he said.

"He's gone?" Marcy asked.

"He sure is." Phil stepped from his hiding place. He stood scratching his head and studying the embankment on both sides. "He couldn't have climbed up."

Marcy hesitated but moved out into the open. She almost relaxed enough to giggle at the thought of that old man climbing the ravine wall.

"Come on, let's look down this way."

"Phil, I think we'd better get out of here."

"Don't worry, we will, just as soon as I find out how Mr. Crowe got out."

Marcy followed her brother down the tracks. He was walking on the crossties and moving so fast Marcy had to run to keep up. All the while he was examining the side of the ravine below the inn.

"Phil!" Marcy gasped.

"What?" Phil whirled around.

"I forgot to tell you. Last night after you went to sleep, I looked out my window and saw two people walking in the ravine down that way." She pointed ahead.

"Then there *has* to be an exit somewhere."

They moved on, slowing in places to examine the wall of the gorge, covered with small vines and bushes. A big broadleaf vine wound over the other growth and in places hid the earth.

"Look, Phil, there's a path," Marcy said in a hushed voice.

"Good work," Phil whispered back. The praise from her brother boosted Marcy's morale. She searched with him as he followed the path with his eyes.

At the same moment they spotted the door, almost hidden by hanging vines. The old weatherworn green door blended with its surroundings and was hardly noticeable.

"I'll bet it's locked from the inside," Phil whispered.

"Don't try it!" Marcy begged. "Let's go. Please, Phil." If Mr. Crowe appeared at that door, she'd die in her tracks. Her knees felt weak. If they waited much longer, she'd never make it up that embankment.

Phil stepped back and looked up at the earth between the door and the old inn. "That means this house has rooms below ground level," he mused.

"I'm going, Phil." Marcy started backing away from the door. The thought of a key turning in the lock and Mr. Crowe stepping out chilled her to the bone. She squinched her eyes as Phil tried the handle.

"Okay, I'm coming, but I'm not forgetting that door. That's for sure."

Phil found the place where they had

climbed down, and they started their ascent. Much to Marcy's surprise, pulling herself up wasn't nearly as difficult as the trip down.

She stayed close behind Phil until they reached the top. Walking into the inn, Marcy asked, "Are you going to tell Mom and Dad about the door?"

"Not yet—and don't you tell them! We'll have to explore from the inside, and they may not let us do that."

Marcy was annoyed that Phil implied she couldn't keep secrets. But his last words quickly pushed that thought from her mind. *Explore from the inside* he said. Marcy's heart skipped a beat.

6.
Making Friends

Marcy didn't have to worry right away about keeping quiet about the door in the ravine. Mr. Dunlap came in at noon excited over the *marvelous* collection of old newspapers at the library. And Mrs. Dunlap had found the librarian, Miss Pettus, to be *one of the most delightful persons* she had ever met. They were both eager to talk about their morning.

"And just think, Tom," Mrs. Dunlap said, "they've been looking for a substitute librarian for the summer."

"You're going to do it then?" Mr. Dunlap asked.

Mrs. Dunlap's brown eyes twinkled. She shared her husband's love for books. "If there are no objections. It's close to the apartment, and the children love to read."

Marcy opened her mouth to speak, then

hesitated and looked at Phil. She knew they must not appear too enthusiastic over their mom's working. She might suspect they wanted her away from the apartment.

Taking the cue, Phil said, "It's okay by me."

"Yeah, Mom, Phil and I will be okay." Marcy added. "We'll read and . . . and . . . gee, that ravine is cool." She looked at Phil to see if she had said too much.

"I noticed your shoes were all smudged from the railroad," Mrs. Dunlap said. Then she smiled.

"We've been walking the rails," Phil admitted.

"And did you know, my offspring," Mr. Dunlap said in his most theatrical voice, "that you were walking right on history itself?

"The railroad through Aiken carried the first steam locomotive in regular passenger service in the United States. It ran from Charleston to a little town on the South Carolina side of the Savannah River called Hamburg—a town with one of the most fascinating histories you've ever heard."

"Do you mean that's the track the Best Friend ran on?" Phil asked. "I studied that in social studies."

"Unfortunately," Mr. Dunlap said, "I don't think the Best Friend got as far as Aiken. From what I've read, it was still on a trial run near Charleston, South Carolina, when a fireman became annoyed by the noise of the escaping steam and sat on the safety valve. He was killed instantly and the Best Friend was almost destroyed."

"How terrible!" said Mrs. Dunlap.

"Yes, it was," Mr. Dunlap agreed. "The train was rebuilt, but they changed its name to Phoenix.

"Of course, the original track wasn't the one down in this ravine. It ran through what is now known as Hitchcock Woods. You see, Aiken is on a hill and the train engine didn't have the power to climb steep grades. Later, this deep gorge was cut."

Marcy saw her brother's eyes light up. Like their father, Phil had a real interest in history. "That track was pretty long for those days, wasn't it, Dad?"

"Yes—136 miles, to be exact."

"How fast do you think it went?" Phil asked.

"Oh, fifteen to twenty-five miles an hour, and they thought that was really traveling." Mr.

Dunlap smiled. "The passengers rode in open coaches, and the smoke from the stack left them blackened with soot and ashes."

"Miss Pettus said an old legend attributes a romance for the railroad being laid through Aiken rather than some other place," Mrs. Dunlap said.

Mr. Dunlap laughed. "Oh, you women are such romantics."

"*Really!* I'm serious." Mrs. Dunlap was excited now, and Marcy and Phil, caught up in the story, forgot about Mr. Crowe and the ravine.

"She said you may not find it recorded, but it was rumored the girl's father, Captain W. W. Williams, would not approve his daughter Sarah's marriage unless the railroad came through Aiken."

"And what does rumor say her young suitor's name was?" Mr. Dunlap teased.

"Dexter. Alfred A. Dexter—a young civil engineer from Boston who helped to lay out the route of the railroad. He boarded at the Williamses' home, which incidentally was the first home built in Aiken. And, it still stands not far from Whiskey Road."

"If he brought the railroad here, why wasn't the town named for him?" asked Phil.

"Because it was named for the man who made the railroad possible, an Irishman who came to America when he was eight years old: William Aiken. He was the leader of those who wanted the railroad built and president of Carolina Railroad and Canal Company."

"Oh, dear, it's almost two o'clock," Mrs. Dunlap said, jumping up from the table.

The frightening experience of the morning suddenly ran through Marcy's mind, and she thought of what Phil said about going *inside* the old inn. A shiver ran down her spine.

Mrs. Dunlap noticed the change on her daughter's face. "Marcy, don't you feel well?"

Before Marcy could answer, her father said, "They probably played too hard this morning. A trip to the library should calm them down a bit."

"Yeah," said Phil. "A trip to the library will cure almost anything, won't it, Dad?"

A trip to the library it was. . . . Not that Phil and Marcy didn't enjoy libraries—they were brought up in them—but just now something else held their attention. For the time being, however, their new adventure would have to wait.

On the way to the library Phil asked his dad

about his trip to the realtor's office.

"Mr. Beard said to ignore the poor old fellow," Mr. Dunlap answered. "You were right, Phil. He is eccentric."

Mrs. Dunlap kept up her husband's brisk pace. "Miss Pettus said for years the townspeople tried to be nice to the Crowes, especially after the inn closed. But the couple was just plain standoffish—or, rather, *he* was. No one seems to know much about his wife, except that her mother was 'society' from Philadelphia and married a Southern gentleman. Mrs. Crowe's family, it's told, disowned her when she married her riding instructor."

Marcy's jaw dropped. "Mr. Crowe was a riding instructor?" She couldn't picture that crabby old man as any kind of teacher. And she had to stifle a laugh imagining him on a horse.

"Well, whatever he was," Mr. Dunlap said, "I can't understand how anyone can be so ill-tempered and live with himself."

"Neither can I," Mrs. Dunlap agreed. "Miss Pettus said for the last five or six years he's lived almost like a hermit."

The woods on their right were teeming with feathered and furry inhabitants. Birds fluttered from branch to branch, chirping. Squirrels scampered up tree trunks and chased each other on the ground. Marcy thought it seemed a nice place to sit in the cool and daydream. Before the summer ended, she would try it, she promised herself.

They could see the library now. An enormous shaggy dog lay on the sidewalk just outside the door, waiting for his master. As they reached the library entrance, the dog lifted his head and wagged his tail.

When the Dunlaps entered the library, a petite woman scurried from behind the oval circulation desk to greet them. Marcy noticed the hollows and shadows in the lady's face . . . *maybe she didn't get enough to eat.* A silver chain attached to eyeglasses hung around a neck so thin it reminded Marcy of a baby bird stretching for food.

"This must be Marcia and Philip," the lady beamed, holding out a bony hand to each of them.

"Yes," Mrs. Dunlap said. Then, turning to Marcy and Phil, "And, children, this is Miss Pettus, the librarian."

Marcy knew why her mother called Miss Pettus delightful. Her blue eyes twinkled, and she spoke like a storyteller sharing a tall tale.

Marcy liked her already.

"Mr. Dunlap," Miss Pettus said, "your nook is waiting. I've put some new material there for you."

"Great!" Forming a circle in the air with his thumb and forefinger, he headed for the stacks.

Mrs. Dunlap walked behind the desk as Miss Pettus ushered Phil and Marcy to a table where a tanned, dark-haired boy was reading.

"Jerry," she said, "I want you to meet Philip and Marcia Dunlap. They're here for the summer and living at the old Telfair Inn."

Marcy thought she saw Jerry stiffen when Miss Pettus mentioned the inn.

"Jerry's sister is about your age, Marcy," Miss Pettus continued. "She's at camp this week, but I'm sure you'll enjoy meeting each other when she returns. Make yourselves at home now."

Miss Pettus turned to resume her duties as a mother with two small children entered the library. She walked over to welcome them, using the excited storytime voice Marcy had already come to enjoy.

Noticing Jerry's book, Phil said, "*The Ghost Cadet* — I've read that. It's good." He and Marcy sat down at the table.

Jerry marked his place and closed the book. Squirming in his chair, he said in a soft drawl, "It's okay. I don't like to read too much, but I'm in the summer reading club. This is on the list." Then he grinned. "The teacher'll give me an extra A next year for joining the club."

Marcy was about to get up to look for a book when Jerry asked, "Do you *really* live at the inn?"

"Since yesterday," Phil answered.

"Have you seen old man Crowe?"

Marcy opened her mouth to speak, but Phil was too fast. "Yeah, we've seen him," he said. And his look told Marcy they shouldn't say too much.

"Scarey old man, isn't he?" Jerry frowned.

"Yeah, he didn't want us to live there," Phil replied.

"He doesn't like kids. You know that cane he carries?" Jerry leaned closer as if he were about to divulge a secret.

"Yeah," Phil and Marcy said together.

"He doesn't really need it. He just has it to chase kids with."

Goosebumps rippled Marcy's arms. She relived the morning's episode when Mr. Crowe was headed down the ravine toward them.

"Some people say that old inn's haunted," Jerry continued.

Marcy was dying to find out if Jerry knew about the door in the ravine wall. "There sure are a lot of birds in this town," she heard Phil say. She knew her brother was changing the subject because he thought she might slip up and give away their secret.

"Yeah, it's against the law to shoot one," Jerry said.

Marcy had the feeling if it weren't against the law, Jerry would enjoy shooting them.

"Is that your dog outside?" she asked.

Jerry nodded his head and grinned, "Yep, that's Shep. Follows me everywhere I go. He gives the teachers a fit when school's in."

The three of them laughed.

"Well, see you later," Phil said as he headed for the stacks.

Marcy walked toward the oval desk, where her mother was helping a young reader make a selection.

Jerry let out a long sigh and opened his book again.

Like her parents, Marcy loved a library. She liked its smell: a mixture of old leather, paste, newsprint, and oil from the wood floor. The odors were familiar and comforting to her.

For the next few hours Phil and Marcy browsed in the stacks, read, and listened while their father told them more local history and showed them pictures. To take back to the apartment, Phil checked out a book on South Carolina birds and Marcy chose *Witch of Blackbird Pond.*

The afternoon seemed to pass in a flash and before they knew it, the library doors were locked and they were headed back to the inn.

As Marcy helped her mother prepare dinner, they talked of the events of the afternoon. That evening Marcy sat at the tall mahogany secretary and wrote Ellen a long letter.

7.
Trespassing

When Marcy awoke the next morning to yellow sunlight streaking across her floor, she knew she had slept later than she meant. Today promised too much excitement to sleep.

She slipped on an old pair of cut-off jeans and a striped T-shirt. She gave her hair a hasty brushing before catching it up in a rubber band, brushed her teeth in a rush, and ran downstairs. Even though she was still uneasy over the prospect of going inside the deserted part of the inn, her curiosity outweighed her fear.

When she bounced down the stairs, her parents were still at the breakfast table, drinking coffee and reading the newspaper. Marcy poured herself a bowl of cereal with milk and ate so fast it didn't have time to get soggy. Then, as quick as a flash she dashed outside to join Phil.

Within minutes after their parents left for

the library, Marcy and Phil were stepping cautiously over uneven gray stones toward the forbidden section of the inn. The short boulevard bordering that side of the building was deserted.

"Are we really going inside?" Marcy asked.

"Of course."

"But, Phil, there's a sign." Marcy pointed to a weathered board nailed to the side of the building. The warning NO TRESPASSING! was scrawled in crude hand printing.

Jerry's remark, "Some people say that old inn is haunted," still rang in Marcy's ears.

Vines tangled in broken windows, and old bricks and boards lay heaped in piles. Phil wasted no time. He edged toward the building and squeezed himself between loose boards.

"Come on." He waved his arm to motion Marcy to follow. She hesitated.

"If you're chicken," he taunted, "you don't have to come."

Marcy's temper flared just enough to give her courage. "I'm not chicken," she snapped. "It's just that Mom and Dad wouldn't like it one little bit if they knew." Getting no response from her brother, she took a deep breath and inched her way into the opening after him.

"This must be where the razing crew

started," Phil said over his shoulder.

Thankful their rubber-soled sneakers made little noise, they stepped carefully into an enormous room. They could see this had been the original front entrance. A desk, like one in a hotel, stood beneath dust-covered mailboxes. Cobwebs hung from the ceiling.

They crept into an adjoining room. Shreds of rotted draperies sagged from broken, dirty French windows lining the outside wall. Through the windows they caught glimpses of a stone terrace half hidden by a broadleaf vine.

"This must have been the dining room," whispered Marcy.

Stepping with caution on the rotted floor, they crossed into another room as large as the dining room. Dirt dauber nests clung to the corners. A huge fireplace with blackened stones added a faint smell of ash to the dusty room. Above the fireplace, the mantel looked heavy with dust. It had been many years since a fire sparked onto the hearth below. A spider crawled up the wall toward a big cobweb draped from the high ceiling to one end of the mantel. The creepy feeling Marcy had when she first entered the inn grew worse.

As they made their way through the tangle

of splintered lumber and broken plaster, Marcy tried to imagine the rooms furnished in the elegant style of their apartment.

Phil picked his way through the heaps of rubble on the floor and entered a hallway leading to another wing of the old building. Marcy followed close like his shadow. Their footsteps caused the old wood floors to creak and groan.

It was darker in the hallway, and dust motes danced in the pale light filtering in from a window at the far end.

Marcy held her breath as Phil tried to open one of the many doors. Creaking in complaint, the old door swung open in slow motion. They saw yet another empty room suffering from neglect.

"There must be two hundred rooms in this place," Phil whispered.

They tiptoed to the end of the hallway, where a spiral staircase, like the one in their apartment, wound downward.

"Maybe this leads to the basement," Phil said.

Marcy opened her mouth to speak, but no words came out. After several tries, she found her voice. "O-Oh, Phil, you're not . . . going down there!"

"Why not?"

Marcy's throat tightened in fear. She was sure her blood had stopped running in her veins. Was Phil as brave as he tried to sound? She was never more frightened in her life. The air was close and musty as they descended the steep, dim staircase.

All of a sudden Phil came to a halt. He could go no farther. The stairwell was boarded up. He darted around Marcy and back up the steps. On the landing, he tripped. Looking down he saw several boards haphazardly nailed over an opening in the floor.

Marcy rushed to Phil's side and watched, shaking, while he knelt and took a firm grip of a large plank. She closed her eyes against the impact. Phil yanked and the board cracked loose. A cloud of dust spiraled.

When Marcy opened her eyes, Phil had disappeared!

"Phil? Phil? Where are you?" Marcy's voice sounded louder than she intended, startling her. She swung her arms frantically at the enveloping dust.

Like a voice rising from a dark pit, Phil's answer came from somewhere below. "I'm down here," he called.

"In that hole?"

"Yeah, I think it must be an old elevator shaft." His voice echoed in the narrow hole.

"Are you hurt?"

"N-No, I don't think so. I caught onto some old ropes."

"What'll we do now?" Phil had really gone too far this time, as far as Marcy was concerned.

"I see an opening of light," he said. "Come down."

"Come down? How can I?"

"Like you did in the ravine. Turn around backwards. Grab hold one of the ropes and let your feet follow it down. Come on. I'll guide you."

Knowing Phil would never turn back now, Marcy took a shaky breath and turned around to let herself down. As she clung for dear life, the rope swung slightly, bumping her against the wall. Finally she made it to the bottom.

As she let go of the rope, she felt Phil's hand clamp hard over her mouth. Luckily she saw it coming or it would have scared the daylights out of her.

"S-s-h-h-h! Be still. Listen!" he said.

They held their breath. A low crooning, like someone singing, came from the other side of the wall. Then all was quiet. Crouching against the wall, they strained to hear another sound.

Marcy's hand trembled as she brushed the veil of spiderwebs from her hair. She didn't care any more if Phil said she was chicken. "Let's go, Phil, please," she begged. "I'm scared."

"Oh, all right."

Marcy had the feeling Phil wasn't as brave as he pretended.

"Let's see if we can find some stairs," he said. "We're below ground level."

Moving cautiously through the corridor away from the elevator shaft, they came upon another staircase. They rushed up the stairs and down another long hallway.

Marcy felt as if they had been moving in this maze of halls and rooms for hours. She always wanted to explore an old house, but she hadn't known it would be like this. As they zigzagged in an effort to find an exit, it was easy for Marcy to believe this spooky section of the inn really did house ghosts—the kind that wore white sheets, clanked chains, and moaned.

Finally, panting and puffing, they came to a door that led outside. Phil tried the handle. It was locked. Pale and breathless, Marcy trailed her brother through more dust and cobwebs until they saw a shattered window.

"We can climb out here," he said.

Crawling through the vine-covered opening, they found themselves on an aged stone terrace. As soon as they got their bearings, they broke into a run toward the entrance to the apartments. Marcy stumbled and fell once, but she was up again in an instant. They had almost reached the corner of the building when they heard an angry shout behind them. Looking over their shoulders, they saw Mr. Crowe waving his cane in the air.

"Git along!" he bellowed.

Marcy panicked as Phil's strong legs kept him several paces ahead of her. As they rounded the corner to the renovated section, they looked back. The old man was still standing there, glaring after them. He lifted his cane in another gesture of fury.

"What a crab!" Phil panted as they flung themselves on the steps of the veranda.

Marcy's heart pounded. Her legs shook from the hard run and her breath came in short jerks. Tears flooded her eyes. Batting them away, she noticed Phil's freckled face had a sickly green cast beneath the dirt and dust. She knew he was frightened too. She also knew he'd never admit it.

"I don't like him, Phil."

"After this, I don't either."

"He gives me the creeps. I think we better tell Mom and Dad."

"No, Marcy! Don't be a dope. They won't leave us alone anymore if you tell."

"But what if he tells on us?"

"Don't worry. He won't. There's something down there he doesn't want us to know about, and if he tells, it'll make him look suspicious. He won't tell."

"I hope you're right." Marcy had doubts. Then she had a frightening thought. "Phil, we might be in danger."

"As long as we stay out of the old man's way, we're not in danger. That's all we gotta do—stay out of Mr. Crowe's way."

8.
Wild Goose Chase

"Who's ready for a wild goose chase?" Mr. Dunlap asked at the breakfast table.

When Mr. Dunlap was engaged in research, he was always ready for what his family called a "wild goose chase." The family would pile into the car and drive over the countryside in search of historical markers and sites to verify information he had found in old newspapers and letters. His dream, as his family knew well, was to discover something not yet recorded in history books.

Today was a perfect day for a wild goose chase. The weather was sunny and Mrs. Dunlap had the day off from the library. Phil was always ready to join his father in these searches.

As for Marcy, she was glad to get away

from the inn. After the fright of the day before, she was happy to be included in quiet activity. Several times she had to bite her tongue to keep from telling her parents about yesterday's adventure. She didn't want to take the chance of running into Mr. Crowe any time soon!

With partial directions, Mr. Dunlap left Aiken by way of Pine Log Road and headed toward Augusta, Georgia.

"This road was a famous Tory trail to Fort Moore during the Revolutionary War," he told his family." In fact, it was when this trail was being established that a huge pine fell across the South Edisto River, forming a natural bridge and giving the road its name."

"How fascinating!" said Mrs. Dunlap.

"Where are we going first, Dad?" asked Marcy.

"I thought we'd explore around a famous old dueling ground called Sand Bar Ferry."

"Great!" said Phil. "I read a book about dueling in England. They used swords."

"Even back then there were laws to prevent dueling, but these affairs were kept secret," Mr. Dunlap said.

"You mean they had duels in this country?" asked Marcy, bouncing in her seat.

"Sit still, will you!" griped Phil.

That's the bad thing about older brothers, Marcy thought, they're too bossy.

"To answer your question, Marcy," Mr. Dunlap said, "people who came to this country brought their customs with them. There were still those, especially among the aristocracy, who believed wounded honor could be healed only with blood. In this country, though, the weapons were nearly always pistols."

"I'm glad we're at least a little more civilized now," said Mrs. Dunlap. "Think how much heartache and grief that must have caused."

"Why would a dueling ground be called a ferry?" Phil asked.

Well-researched as usual, Mr. Dunlap was ready with the answer. "It was named for the ferry that crossed the Savannah River. You see, there was a level sandbar on the Georgia side that ran along the river and into the woods. South Carolinians dueled there and then crossed the state line by ferry before the constables from Georgia could arrest them."

"That was sneaky!" said Phil.

"The Georgians did the same," Mr. Dunlap replied. "They dueled on the South Carolina side, on a high bluff where Fort Moore was situated in colonial days. Then the parties would cross by ferry back to Georgia for the same reason."

"Parties?" Marcy asked.

"That means the two principals engaged in the conflict. Present at the duals were two seconds, a surgeon, and sometimes a few friends."

"I still think it's gruesome," said Mrs. Dunlap. "It shouldn't have been permitted."

"You remember," said Mr. Dunlap, "I said it was a *gentleman*'s way of settling an insult. A gentleman of the Old South could never allow himself to be perceived a coward. Many people, especially northerners, felt as you do about dueling. Of course, some southerners were not in favor of the practice either. But even the governor of South Carolina felt if an individual was deeply wronged, he should deal with it in the manner of a gentleman—that meant dueling. The challenge to a duel was an equally serious affair. It was always presented formally in writing."

"It's still astonishing the leaders of a state would condone such barbarism," insisted Mrs. Dunlap.

"Why, in 1838," Mr. Dunlap said, "Governor Wilson of South Carolina compiled a code of honor for duelers to follow. According to his code, one man was never allowed to take unfair advantage of the other. No fight was ever to continue after one man was wounded."

"Is the ferry still there?" Marcy asked, afraid of being bored further with details of the code of honor.

"Probably not. . . . Well, we're here," said Mr. Dunlap, pulling off the highway beside the Sand Bar Ferry Bridge.

As the four climbed from the car, they could see the muddy waters of the Savannah churning swiftly over great rocks, on its way to the Atlantic Ocean. They walked onto the Carolina side of the bridge, where they found a plaque. Mr. Dunlap read the legend of the bridge aloud. Then he recorded it in his little black notebook.

> This bridge, erected upon the site of the old Sand Bar Ferry, stands as a memorial to a spot famous in the history of Georgia and South Carolina.
>
> The ferry served as a crossing place and medium of communication between the peoples of these two great states.

This spot has been the rendezvous for settlements of affairs of honour, which were the topics of toasts of many tales told in vengeful mien, or whispered in bated breath, while hearts have ached and burst with grief.

The raging waters of the Savannah have washed away the blood stains from the sands which around are smiling through the dew, where tears once trembled on the grass. Progress, young and strong has subdued these evils dark, and those tragic scenes have passed into oblivion, save for faint memory and old folk tales.

Back in their car, the Dunlaps crossed the Savannah River into Georgia and headed toward the city of Augusta.

In Augusta they located Magnolia Cemetery, where they visited the tomb of the last known young man to die in a duel at Sand Bar Ferry.

Phil was first to see the grave, so he read the inscription, "Charles Dawson Tilly, December 17, 1875. Tragically killed in the last duel fought at Sand Bar Ferry."

Afterward they walked among the old

gravestones, then they climbed back into the car. Crossing the Savannah River by way of the Fifth Street Bridge, they returned to South Carolina.

"Remember my telling you the railroad ran from Charleston to Hamburg?" Mr. Dunlap pointed to a site on the right. "That small building sitting in the valley is all that's left of Hamburg."

"That sounds German," Mrs. Dunlap said.

"It is," Mr. Dunlap answered. "It seems that Henry Shultz, a poor German immigrant, came to Augusta in 1806. He became a boatman on the Savannah River and saved money to buy a flatboat. While he was working this boat between Augusta and the city of Savannah, he had the idea of building a bridge across the river. In 1814 he built Fifth Street Bridge, the one we just crossed. He and his partners made it a toll bridge, and he became wealthy almost overnight.

"Next he built a bank, called the Bridge Bank, since it was located near the river and his bridge. This bank made its own currency: 'bridge bills.' Everything Henry Schultz touched seemed to turn to money.

"An old newspaper article I read says resentment sprang up against him among the people of Augusta, who called him 'the Dutchman.' At any rate, Shultz decided to return to his native Hamburg in Germany."

As Mr. Dunlap maneuvered through the heavy workday traffic he watched for landmarks.

"Schultz never made it home," he continued. "Agreements he made had not been put in writing and his partners somehow forced him to close the bank. Schultz was suddenly bankrupt.

"Bitter, he crossed the river to the Carolina side and built a town to spite the people of Augusta. He swore he'd ruin the town that ruined him. In 1827 the town of Hamburg was chartered. Schultz offered lower rates for everything and drew Augusta's trade. By 1835 Hamburg was booming, and Shultz was rich again."

Her dad's ability to remember dates had always amazed Marcy. She found it hard even to recall the birthdates of those in her family. She started to comment on it just as her mother said, "So he accomplished what he set out to do."

"But the story doesn't end there," Mr. Dunlap responded.

"I like happy endings, Dad," said Marcy. She could have added that she'd also heard enough of this Shultz fellow, but she knew her dad was intent on finishing.

"So do I, Marcy, but in 1853 a railway bridge across the Savannah River brought doom to Hamburg. The railroad, instead of the river, began to haul freight. With that and the Civil War, Hamburg failed as a town. Before long, Shultz died a penniless man.

"Even the location of his grave is unknown. Wherever it is, legend has it he requested to be buried upright with his back to Augusta, the town he hated to the very end."

"How sad," said Mrs. Dunlap.

As they started back to the inn, Marcy reviewed their day. They had not seen a ferry or a dueling ground. And nothing of note was left of Hamburg. But it had been a good day for her dad, and she was proud for him. His research helped others learn about the past.

That night in bed, Marcy realized another summer day had slipped away. She had come to love this bedroom, with its window overlooking the ravine. But tonight her eyes were heavy. Phil would have to hurry to beat her to sleep. Tomorrow she'd ask Dad what the people did when the Bridge Bank, that printed their money, went broke.

She glanced over at her brother. Darn Phil's time! she thought. He's asleep already.

She propped up on her elbows for one last peek out the window. As usual, the night was shrill with insects. Clouds drifted across the moon. Off in the distant sky a star fell and Marcy made a quick wish.

She was just working up a good yawn when she caught sight of a shadow moving outside the ground floor of the inn. Like the workmen across the street, the figure wore a metal helmet that caught and reflected the moonlight. It looked like a man, tall and thin. What was he doing there? And at this hour of night? He was moving toward the old part of the inn.

Marcy wished Phil were awake. She glanced over at her brother. When she looked back, the figure in the metal hat had disappeared into the night. Within seconds, Marcy was fast asleep.

9.
A Time to Dream

Early the next morning Marcy told Phil about seeing the man in the hardhat snooping around the old section of the inn.

"What did he look like?" Phil asked.

"It was dark and I was looking down on him." She frowned in thought. "He was tall and thin. And he was hunched over like a question mark."

"It must have been one of the workmen across the street," Phil said.

"I'm gonna tell Dad."

"No, Marcy, listen—are you brave enough to go through with this or not?"

"Yes, but—"

"Okay. Then keep quiet until we find out what the old man's hiding. That prowler must think he's hiding something too. You know Dad will make us stop if he finds out."

"Well—all right." Marcy was curious too, but she was not as daring as Phil.

As soon as their parents left for the library, Phil and Marcy headed for the bridge. From that vantage point they could see the workmen as they moved about on the construction site of the new apartment building.

Marcy was glad now that she hadn't waked Phil. For once, her brother needed her. This was one mystery she alone could solve. They sat for awhile on the rail of the bridge with Phil asking repeatedly if she saw the man. "Is that the one? The one next to the work trailers?"

"No."

"How about the one by the crane?"

"No. He's too fat."

"That guy on the crossbeam over there?"

"Umm . . . no."

Marcy realized her brother was growing impatient.

"Well, Phil, I can't help it. It was night."

"Yeah, yeah," he said, jumping down from the bridge rail. "Next time, wake me up, will you?"

"Where are you going?" she asked as he

started across the bridge.

"To see if Jerry's in the library." Phil leaned down to pick up a small stone and, straightening, he hurled it into the ravine.

"Tell Mom I'll be right over here." Marcy pointed to the edge of the woods just over the bridge. "I'll be making honeysuckle garlands."

Forgetting Phil's disappointment in her for being unable to identify the prowler, she wandered to the edge of the woods skirting the far side of the ravine. This was the spot she watched from her bedroom window each night, the place where moonlight made shadows and fireflies danced.

Marcy moved a short way into the growth of long-needled pines, gnarled magnolias, and Carolina cherries. Colorful vines grew in profusion at the base of the forest. It was hard to believe the library was such a short distance away.

She sat down on a low, curving tree limb and looked about. Insects flitted through the air, buzzing, and crickets chirped. In a nearby sparkleberry tree a pair of birds warbled as the morning sunlight dappled the high branches. In the distance, across the ravine, she could hear a workman shout above the whir of machinery and another shout back. But here, sheltered among the trees, was a little private world.

Leaves fluttered as a faint wind breathed overhead. Puffs of white cloud floated far above the treetops.

A sting on her ankle brought Marcy out of her reverie. Slapping at the pain, she looked down to find one foot in the path of a train of tiny orange ants. She squatted to watch them. Laboring after their leader, the ants scuttled up and down little passageways and over layers of leaves as if driven by an unseen force. Marcy leaned against the trunk of a tree and fell into a happy daydream.

Her attention was diverted by a low hum. Turning, she saw a tiny ruby-throated bird darting from blossom to blossom on the honeysuckle vine. The rapid beating of its wings made a humming sound as it glided up and down the vine. Marcy marveled as the bird stopped in midair, then darted backwards.

"Oh, I know," she said aloud, "that's a hummingbird. There's one in Phil's book."

As the bird hummed away, Marcy began breaking off stems of trailing honeysuckle and yellow jessamine. When she had pinched off an armful of vines, she moved to the edge of the ravine and dropped to the ground. A soft breeze brushed her face. Across the ravine, sunlight seemed to set the windows of the sprawling old inn on fire.

From her post at the edge of the woods, Marcy had a clear view of the bridge, in case Phil should return. Crossing her legs Indian style, she sat weaving the vines into a garland for her neck. It was cool in the shade of the trees, but down in the ravine heat shimmered in little wavy patterns above the railroad track.

Out of the corner of her eye, Marcy saw a movement at the bottom of the gorge. Rising just enough to get a good view, she saw Mr. Crowe coming out of the secret door. The sight of him scattered her thoughts like frightened birds. He looked all around, fumbled with the lock, and let the vines fall over the door. Carrying a brown paper bag, he hobbled up the ravine. Even from this distance his presence made Marcy's heart beat faster.

She hurried to finish her wreath of flowers, then followed the road to the library. After the shade of the woods, she blinked against the glaring sunlight.

A line of people waited at the circulation desk. Mrs. Dunlap looked up as Marcy passed. Marcy gave her mom a quick wave in exchange

for a smile. Holding the garland close, Marcy headed toward her father's nook.

"Hi, Sweetie," Mr. Dunlap said as she approached. "What have you there?"

In answer Marcy put the wreath of flowers around her neck. The reddish honeysuckle blooms had wilted, and her lei wasn't as pretty as she'd envisioned it.

"That's nice," he said. "I'm glad you came up. I was just thinking of walking into town. I've been reading about the battle of Aiken during the Civil War. Until today, I didn't know there was one."

"Where's Phil?" Marcy asked.

"He's with Jerry. Just you and I'll go. Okay?"

"Okay." Marcy grinned. Already she felt better, in spite of Mr. Crowe and the wilting garland. She loved going places with her dad—just the two of them.

After whispering their destination to Mrs. Dunlap, they were off. While they walked the short distance, her father told her about the battle of Aiken.

"Were many soldiers killed?" asked Marcy.

"The Confederates lost eight and the Federals twelve. But from what I've read, the

South—especially South Carolina—thinks the North treated them very badly.

"The dead from both the North and the South are buried in cemeteries here. The newspapers said the Daughters of the Confederacy honor them all with flowers each Memorial Day."

In the parkway across the street from the Baptist church a monument honored those killed in war. Mr. Dunlap snapped a picture of it, then they crossed to the marker, where he read the inscription aloud. The Confederates won the battle and kept Aiken and Augusta from being destroyed. Marcy could scarcely take in all the details of generals, cavalry, and infantry.

On the other side of the boulevard, ancient black-trunked magnolias shaded graves. Marcy had been in many old cemeteries with her dad. Something about them calmed her. She felt a reverence for these people who had lived their entire lives before she was born. Her dad said graveyards tell a lot about people—about their battles, their family history, and their sorrows.

Marcy wandered among the graves. How different old cemeteries were from modern ones. She liked to read the inscriptions on the headstones. Her dad studied history that way, but

Marcy liked to daydream about the people buried there. She could tell a lot about them by what was inscribed on their tombstones.

Leaning over a grave she blew away bits of sand and tiny sticks covering the marker. She read,

> *Dearest One*
> *Thou hast left us*
> *Yet again we hope to meet thee*
> *When the day of life is fled*
> *When in heaven with joy to greet thee*
> *Where no farewell tear is shed.*

Mr. Dunlap called for Marcy to come see where the soldiers were buried. A little American flag waved on each marked grave and on the grave of the unknown soldier.

They walked on.

Many of the gravestones they passed were blackened with age and covered with moss. Some sunk low into the earth.

A tiny grave in the distance caught Marcy's attention. She walked over to kneel beside it. A rose sculpted in pink granite marked the grave. The rose petals seemed almost real.

Marcy could tell it was the grave of a small

child. There was no inscription on the stone, but just below the flower was engraved, *OUR ROSE.* How sad the parents must have been to lose their baby. She would ask her mother if one day she could put flowers on the infant's grave.

Marcy and her dad spent almost an hour studying inscriptions and dates. They stopped to admire the beautiful stained-glass windows in the old church before starting back.

A short detour took them by a corner drugstore where they waited at the old-fashioned counter for two strawberry ice cream cones. Taking the shady side of the street, they walked along munching their cones.

10.
The Secret
of the Inn

In spite of trips to the library and historical jaunts with their dad, Marcy and Phil did their best to keep up with Mr. Crowe's comings and goings.

They discovered that when the old man came out of the secret door and hobbled up the railroad track, he was gone at least an hour, sometimes longer. Marcy and Phil watched him time and again, and they decided it was on these trips that he got his provisions. Somewhere out of sight down the track there must be a store, for he always returned with a brown paper bag like one from a grocery.

It was during one of Mr. Crowe's trips that Phil decided it was time to venture again inside the deserted part of the inn. Their parents were sure to be at the library all afternoon. Though Marcy was dying to know the source of the crooning they heard, she felt a chill at the thought of trespassing.

Long rays of light played across the outside wall of the inn as they slipped around to the side bordering the boulevard.

When they reached the narrow, splintered opening and squeezed through, fear knotted Marcy's stomach. She tiptoed behind Phil as he attempted to find the gaping hole they'd gone down before—the one that long ago housed an elevator.

"Do we have to go down that way again, Phil?" Marcy questioned, her mouth already tasting the dust.

"That was where we heard the noise, and I'm not sure of getting to it another way."

The passageway was dim, and cobwebs played with their hair as they walked.

Phil whispered, "Catch hold of this rope."

Marcy turned up her nose. "It smells musty."

"Oh, for crying out loud, just grab hold."

Marcy clenched her teeth and did what he said. Soon Phil was beside her in the dim basement.

They stood with their ears pressed against the wall in the semi-darkness, listening. Marcy hoped there would be no sound from the other side. What if there really were ghosts here? What would they do? How would they ever be able to get away in the maze of hallways?

After what seemed an eternity, they heard a creak. And then it began — the low crooning they'd heard before.

Marcy's heart pounded against the wall of her chest. As she stood in silent misery, she watched Phil, his red hair black in the dim light. Like a detective in a movie he felt along the wall with open palms and tapped his fingers on the wooden panels here and there.

This can't be real! Marcy thought.

She felt the sudden urge to run, when a panel swung open. In the faint light, with no handle on their side, they hadn't realized it was a door. They were startled to see the silhouette of a small, elderly woman appear in the doorway.

"Come in," she called in a tiny voice, no more than a whisper.

The story of Hansel and Gretel flashed through Marcy's mind. She wanted to run, but her feet were stone. Phil, too, was dumbfounded.

So this was what Mr. Crowe had not wanted anyone to know! His wife still lived here! But why was he hiding her? Why was he keeping her locked in this cellar room like a prisoner?

"Will you play with me?" The lady's voice was childlike and pleading.

Marcy and Phil looked at each other bewildered. But before they realized it, they were following her into a room lighted by kerosene lamps. Eerie shadows played on the walls around them. There were no windows to let in the summer heat, so the room was cool. The musty odor that filled this old section of the inn was overpowered in this room by the sweet fragrance of lilac.

The lady closed the door and with a faraway look she said to Marcy, "Why, you're Rose."

"No, ma'm," answered Marcy in a shaky voice. "I'm Marcy Dunlap from New York, and this is my brother Phil. We're staying at the inn."

"Oh." The lady's face drooped. The next instant, it brightened as she asked, "Have you been to a party in the great ballroom yet?"

"No, ma'm—"

Before Marcy could finish answering, Phil

nudged her. Marcy knew that meant be quiet. "She's senile, like Aunt Clara," he whispered.

When Marcy looked again at the little woman, she was seated in a wicker rocker in the center of the room holding a doll. She was rocking, smiling, and crooning. *So this was what they heard!*

The knot of fear in Marcy's stomach began to loosen as she watched the woman's face. Her features were dainty, and her faded blue eyes looked right past them. She sat erect in her chair, rocking . . . rocking. Her small wrinkled fingers stroked the doll's cracked plaster head with tenderness.

Phil and Marcy looked around the room. The space had once been a wine cellar. Racks where bottles were stored now held colorful little trinkets, artificial flowers, and department-store souvenirs.

On a marble-topped table a tarnished golden frame displayed a picture of a smiling, handsome couple. The girl was beautiful, with short golden curls. Dressed in riding clothes, she sat on a well-groomed horse and smiled down at the young man holding the reins. The photograph was signed in a bottom corner, "To Lillian with all my love, Your husband, Silas."

"Why, that's Mr. Crowe!" Marcy heard herself say aloud. She couldn't believe it was possible. The lady in the picture had the same sweet face as the old lady in the rocker. Incredible! But hadn't Mom said she married her riding instructor, and her family had disapproved? Marcy motioned Phil over to look.

It was impossible for them to take everything in. As Mrs. Crowe sat arranging and rearranging the doll's long white dress, Phil and Marcy continued to look about them. Relics of long ago cluttered the room. Screens with colorful designs divided the area into kitchen, bedroom, and sitting room. Marcy could see a two-burner oil stove behind one screen. Cardboard boxes filled with clothing and other items rose like a pyramid in a corner.

An old-fashioned trunk with an oval lid sat against one wall. The only sound in the room, except for the creaking of the rocker, was the measured tick of an antique clock.

The old woman rose slowly, looking at Marcy and Phil as if she were seeing them for the first time. "Hold my baby," she said to Marcy, "and I'll show you my trunk." She gently handed Marcy the doll, whose face had the same faraway expression as Mrs. Crowe's.

The doll's green glass eyes stared straight ahead, then rolled shut in their loose sockets as Marcy cradled it in her arms.

If there was anything that held more fascination than an old trunk, Marcy couldn't think what it was. She and Phil stooped to see the contents as Mrs. Crowe eased herself down onto a short needlepoint stool.

Phil helped Mrs. Crowe lift the heavy lid. When the trunk was opened, Marcy and Phil strained their necks to see. Mrs. Crowe pulled out an ancient leather Bible with gilt lettering on its worn cover. The back cover had broken loose and she held it in place as she leafed to a certain page.

"That tells who I am," she said. "Sometimes I don't remember, but it's all written down right here." She turned the Bible toward Phil. "Read it to me."

Faltering, he read the spidery writing, "Lillian Lucretia Pinckney, daughter of John Robert Pinckney, Sr., and Lucretia Rose Vincent."

A shadow moved across the old woman's face as she turned to another page. "And this tells of our Rose."

So the tiny grave in the cemetery held the Crowes' baby! A lump formed in Marcy's throat, and she thought she might cry.

"Mrs. Crowe, may I look at this?" Phil pointed to several stacks of money. Marcy had never seen him look so surprised. She knew he was itching to see what else was in the trunk.

Mrs. Crowe picked up a stack of currency and handed it to Phil.

Phil whistled as he flipped the stack of bills and recognized the printing on both sides.

"Say! This is Hamburg bank currency," he cried. "Would Dad like to see this!"

"Is it still good, Phil?"

"Not to spend—but for museums, yes."

Mrs. Crowe seemed not to listen. She was busy opening a slender, carved box. When she lifted the top, Phil and Marcy gasped. There, right before their eyes, lay a handsome pair of pistols. The single-barreled weapons were polished to a high sheen.

"Dueling pistols!" Phil exclaimed in disbelief.

"Yes," Mrs. Crowe said. "Before I was born my grandfather was killed in a duel with one of these pistols."

The old woman seemed almost normal now as she began the story. Yet her frail voice had a distant quality about it.

"The disagreement was over a strip of land adjoining their properties. Here is the challenge."

From the top of the box she removed a yellowed sheet of paper with handwriting so fancy it seemed printed by computer. She handed it to Phil, and he read it aloud.

June 12, 1870

Sir John Robert Pinckney,

I have received your communication of June 5, whereby you state the land along the grey moss oaks belongs to the Pinckney estate. You degrade my character and grossly insult me by suggesting I would use your land as my own.

In the face of such an affront, I challenge you to meet me in the field. You may have the honor of selecting the weapons and time for our meeting in the secluded glade to settle our personal difficulties.

Drayton DuBois Hampton

"Wow!" Marcy squealed, her eyes sparkling. "Dad would flip over this!"

Phil was hardly able to contain himself. Realizing there was writing on the back of the old challenge, he turned the paper over. There in a feminine hand was written,

> *In the prime of life my darling fell a victim to the barbarous practice of dueling.*

"And this is my grandfather's diary," Mrs. Crowe continued, lifting a handsome bound journal onto her lap. "My grandmother gave me all his personal things." She sat silent and drifted once again into her dream world. After a while she looked at Phil, raised her thin eyebrows, and said, "Well, for goodness sake, Thomas Marion, when did you check in?"

Phil stifled a laugh and looked at Marcy. They understood.

The trunk contained many items the two had not yet examined—letters yellowed with age, a tiny gold watch, little trinket boxes, and much more. It was unbelievable! The history packed into this trunk would take their dad's breath away.

They suddenly realized the passage of time and knew they couldn't take the chance of Mr. Crowe's returning to find them there. So Phil and Marcy began replacing the trunk's contents.

Mrs. Crowe crept back to her rocker. "He's going to bring me a present," she said smiling.

"That's nice." Marcy handed the lady her doll, thinking, Poor thing, she doesn't even realize she's being hidden away. Marcy knew now that when Mr. Crowe walked up the railroad track, he always brought his wife a surprise. And all those little trinkets stuck in the wine bottle racks must be the things he brought her. She just couldn't imagine that crabby old man being sweet to anyone.

Phil and Marcy slipped out through the door Mrs. Crowe had opened to them earlier, leaving her there, rocking and crooning.

"Kinda gives you a spooky feeling, doesn't it?" Marcy said.

"When you're alone with them it does—but I guess old age just does that to some people."

"Yeah." Marcy thought again of Great Aunt Clara. When they last visited her, she mistook Phil and Marcy for her children and Mrs. Dunlap for her dead sister. It seemed so sad, but their mother explained that senile people are happy in their dream world—and sometimes it's even a blessing. "When their minds are filled with happy thoughts of the past," Mrs. Dunlap had said, "they're not lonely."

As they searched for an exit, Marcy was amazed at how calm she felt. The house wasn't haunted after all! Telfair Inn *did* have a deep, dark secret, and she and Phil had discovered it. In a way, the inn *had* harbored a ghost. And there *was* a hidden treasure—not a chest with precious stones or gold coins, but a real treasure for a historical researcher. She just *had* to tell Dad!

Marcy's heart beat fast—not from fear this time, but from joy. She knew how happy their dad would be when they gave him the good news. Right here in the inn was evidence to back up his research: money printed by Shultz's bank, dueling pistols and a written challenge, and lots more. And there was no telling what the old journal would reveal.

Long after Phil was asleep that night, Marcy lay awake, putting the pieces of the puzzle together in her mind. Phil had insisted they not tell their parents. If Mrs. Crowe told Mr. Crowe about their visit, Marcy had argued, the cat would be out of the bag. Why did Phil have to be so stubborn! She was furious with him all evening, and she wasn't over it yet.

"No, we can't tell yet, Marcy," he'd said. "Even if Mrs. Crowe says anything, he'll think she's just rambling. You know how she kept thinking we were people she used to know."

Marcy had been so angry with her brother she said terrible things, things she didn't mean. But when she snapped at him that she'd just tell anyway, he called her a baby. That had *really* made her mad!

"If we don't handle it right," he said, "Dad'll never get to see those things. You don't think Mr. Crowe will invite him in, do you? And you know Dad. He'd never do anything sneaky, even for his beloved research."

Phil's arguments always made sense, but she would not give him the satisfaction of telling him so. "All right, Mr. Know-It-All, but I'm not giving you much longer," she declared.

He turned toward the wall muttering, "Aw, drop dead." Before she could think of a good comeback, he was fast asleep. Marcy was left to fume in silence.

Lying in the dark, she thought of Mrs. Crowe. So she was the one Marcy had seen walking in the ravine with Mr. Crowe on their first night at the inn. He couldn't take her for a walk in the daytime because he didn't want anyone to know she was there. Why was her presence such a secret? He must love her to be so good to her, yet he was such a mean old man. Just the thought of him made Marcy shiver.

The song of a mockingbird in the woods across the ravine made its way through Marcy's window. Phil's book said it was the father mockingbird who sang at night.

Listening to the bird and daring to wonder what tomorrow would bring, she finally drifted off to sleep.

11.
Coker Spring

The next morning Marcy felt terrible. She knew when her parents found out what she and Phil had done, they were going to be in real trouble. Phil knew it too. So why put off telling them any longer? What could possibly happen that would make what they did all right? . . . And where was he now, while she was here worrying about it all alone?

Marcy walked out onto the veranda. The sunlight was bright and already hot. She was surprised to see Phil and Jerry and a tanned girl with short, dark hair about her age coming across the bridge. Shep ambled along behind them.

The girl saw Marcy and gave her a big smile. Marcy liked her right away.

"Hey, Marcy," Phil called, "make some peanut butter and jelly sandwiches, would you.

We're all going to Coker Spring. Mom says it's okay."

If Phil remembered their heated quarrel of last night, Marcy thought, his cheerful voice gave no evidence of it.

Inside, making the sandwiches, Marcy learned that the girl's name was Sarah and she was Jerry's sister, the one Miss Pettus told her about. She also learned that the pack on Jerry's back contained four drinks they planned to chill in the icy water of Coker Spring.

The sky was bright blue with billowy white clouds as they made their way to Coker Spring Road. The sun was hot and Marcy's shirt stuck to her back. They left the pavement and began their descent to a dirt road gullied by recent rains. Bared tree roots clung to the edge of the roadbed. Shep ran just ahead of them.

"You can't come down here in a car," Jerry said. "The road's all washed out."

Great trees stretched tall above them. Jerry seemed to know them all. Most of the pale green ones were poplars, he said. Those with red-brown bark were spicy sassafras. Here and there a vine twisted around the trunk of a towering pine like an octopus and burst into bloom at the top of the tree.

As they moved deeper into the forest, oak limbs formed a canopy over the narrow dirt road. Marcy had entered another world, one far away from the inn and Mr. Crowe—one of slender willow trees, trailing arbutus, pokeberry plants, and tiny ferns whose leaves closed when snatched from their marshy bed. Bamboo sprung up between clusters of Carolina cherry trees and blackberry bushes.

"It's like a park," Marcy said, thinking of one they'd visited in upstate New York.

"Yeah," said Jerry, "but a wild one."

Sarah was as game as any to walk through weeds where a snake might be. She'd even be the third one, and Jerry said that's the one a snake will bite if he's going to bite anybody.

The woods had Marcy so entranced they were at the spring before she realized it.

"There it is!" said Jerry in triumph.

Marcy could hear water trickling, but she couldn't see it. The spring was covered with crumbling bricks that formed a little house. Marcy figured the tiny opening on the front must be the place to get water, but she couldn't see the spring.

"Where's the water?" she and Phil asked together. Jerry and Sarah laughed.

"Down here," said Jerry, pointing toward a bed of ferns and wild grapevines, where Shep had already started to drink.

"I don't get it," said Phil.

"This is a horse trail," said Sarah, running on ahead. "They cemented the spring bed to make the water run down here into this trough so the horses can drink when the riders come by."

Placing the drinks into the trough to cool, Jerry said, "Miss Pettus thinks it's terrible. She's a Daughter of the American Revolution, and she thinks historic spots should be preserved. Coker Spring was a chief source of water around the time of the Revolutionary War."

"And," added Sarah, "she says if you drink water from Coker Spring, you'll always come back to Aiken, no matter where you roam." Sarah's dark eyes danced as she waved the others forward with her hand. "So, drink up!"

Stooping at the noisy little cascade, they cupped their hands and sipped the bubbling water. It was cold. Jerry splashed his face and the others copied him. They all laughed, drowning out the water's chorus.

While Shep jumped playfully around them, Jerry and Sarah shared their secret places. Marcy and Phil marveled at the retreat of green frogs and spiders as their world was invaded.

As they romped in this wilderness wonderland, Jerry charmed them with his knowledge of the outdoors. He told them the names of wild flowers and vines, warning them against some, as their father had done. He chanted the age-old jingle, "Leaves of three, let it be!" He whistled to birds and they answered him. They watched a redbird pull his topknot of red over his flat head.

"There's a praying mantis," Jerry whispered.

Camouflaged among the leaves was an insect that looked just like a little old lady at prayer. Its two long forelegs were folded neatly under its bowed head. Its body looked like an old-fashioned skirt.

"That's a cannibal insect," said Phil.

"It doesn't eat people, I hope!" said Marcy. Giggling, she and Sarah backed away.

"Only girls," Phil answered.

"They eat insects," Jerry said, "but they eat the good ones as well as the bad. And sometimes the female mantis even eats the male mantis."

"Hey, be still, you two." Phil frowned at the girls, who were still giggling and jumping around behind them. "You'll scare him away."

They watched in silence as the mantis turned its head in a wide arc, its large compound eyes bulging from the triangular head. Quicker than their eyes could follow, the long arms of the mantis shot out, grabbing its prey, and the mouth devoured it.

"Ooooh!" screamed Marcy and Sarah, frightening the mantis away.

"Shucks!" said Jerry. "Wish I'd had a mason jar. I could've caught him for science. You don't see many of them around."

"Jerry and I used to always keep a jar of tadpoles when we were little," Sarah said. "We liked to watch them turn into frogs. But Mamma made us quit. She said God made 'em to live in ponds and we should leave 'em there."

Jerry pulled out a stubby pocketknife and dug a piece of bark from a sweet gum tree. Then he scraped off the soft inner layer. "This is sapwood," he said. He rolled the sticky sap into four little balls with the palms of his hands. "Here," he said, "chew on this. It works like chewing gum."

"That's cool!" Phil said, taking a piece.

Marcy was doutbtful, even before Sarah said, "Trust me — don't even try it."

The boys chewed, telling the girls, between chomps, how much they were missing. But knowing their brothers pretty well, Marcy and Sarah knew the boys were having a hard time keeping their faces straight.

A little farther on they came to a pasture surrounded by a white wood fence. Reaching between the fence boards, they petted grazing horses whose coats were slick in the sunlight. Shep chased butterflies until the others were ready to move on.

They walked a fallen tree that had lost its battle with the earth. They hung from the limbs of spreading oaks.

"The only thing you can hang from in New York," said Phil, "is a jungle gym."

"Policemen patrol parks just to keep kids out of trees," Marcy added.

Finally they returned to the spring, kicked off their sneakers, and plunged their feet into the icy trough. The others laughed at Marcy's expression when her dangling feet touched the slimy, moss-covered bottom. Drifts of willow leaves floated around wiggling toes. When they could take the cold no longer, they stepped out onto a grassy plot, their feet red and tingly.

Sitting on an old log, they devoured their

sandwiches and cooled drinks. Jerry gave Shep a couple dog biscuits he'd stuck in his pocket.

After they ate, Jerry found a sassafras tree. Whittling away small strips of exposed root, he told them that old-timers used the strips as toothbrushes. Fraying one end of each strip, he fanned it out into soft threads.

"Try it," Jerry said, holding a strip out to each of them. "If the taste is too strong, stick it in the spring." Then he began to rub his own teeth.

The spicy aroma of sassafras filled the air. When Marcy put the root into her mouth, she was surprised to find that it tasted exactly like it smelled. She couldn't tell where smell stopped and taste began.

The sun was low when they started back to the inn, the girls walking arm in arm behind their brothers. As the group trudged up the hill, Jerry carried on a conversation with a bobwhite in the thicket. Of course, all either of them said was "Bobwhite."

When they emerged from the valley and the top of Telfair Inn came into view, Marcy's pleasant thoughts turned sour. For a whole day she forgot about the Crowes! If Phil's mood changed on seeing the inn, he didn't show it. . . . If only he'd agree to share their secret with Jerry and Sarah. After all, they had become good friends. But she knew he would never agree. "Shep would be a dead giveaway in the basement," he'd argue.

With the promise of more happy excursions, Marcy and Phil watched their new summer friends cross the bridge and disappear.

12.
A Terrible Accident

Almost every day for the next week Marcy and Phil slipped in to see Mrs. Crowe. With more time to explore, they found an easier way to get to her basement room than climbing down the elevator shaft. They were careful each visit to leave before it was time for Mr. Crowe to return, but they always had an uneasy feeling they might get caught. Twice they had narrow escapes, and Marcy vowed she would not go again. Yet when the next opportunity presented itself, she couldn't pass it by.

Sometimes they found Mrs. Crowe cheerful and talkative. Other times she would be lost in her dreamworld. One day she didn't remember them at all. At first Marcy was upset, but Phil reminded her of how Aunt Clara had acted.

Both marveled at Mrs. Crowe's clear memories of past events. So many things she told them were right in line with their father's research. Marcy was still dying to tell their secret. And she was determined that somehow her dad would get to see those historical treasures before the summer ended.

"We will, Marcy, I promise," Phil kept saying, "but we gotta find just the right time and do it the right way."

"You think Dad's going to be mad, don't you?" she asked.

"Well, he won't be pleased that we trespassed."

"We've been downright deceitful, Phil, and I feel terrible about it."

"Okay, okay. Maybe tomorrow."

Black clouds edged across the sky just before sundown, and dark came earlier than usual. In bed, Marcy propped up on her pillow and breathed the night air. She had come to look forward to this time. Listening to the crickets, chirping first over here and then over there, she was reminded of a choral reading from her class at school.

Distant rumbles interrupted the crickets' concert, and the wind began to whistle through the bamboo hedge. Marcy imagined she could hear sounds echo in the ravine. Tall pines swayed and an oak limb scraped against the inn with a rasping sound. Loose shutters rattled.

Marcy closed the window just as the night exploded. Silver whips of light tore at the sky. Thunder clapped like cymbals in a marching band. Rain slashed at the window. Marcy lay quiet, listening to the shifting wind as it rushed the rain in torrents, this way and that.

She wasn't afraid of thunderstorms. Since she and Phil were little, they had watched them with their dad. He explained that lightning is just a big spark of electricity jumping from cloud to cloud or from cloud to earth. He let them make their own thunder by blowing up empty paper bags, holding them closed tight, then popping them.

Like many summer storms, the downpour stopped abruptly, as it had begun. Marcy slipped her feet over the side of the bed and pushed open the window.

The sky was brighter now and there was a fresh smell to the air. She closed her eyes and breathed deeply.

Opening her eyes, she caught her breath and ducked back inside the window. Then she rose just enough to peek over the sill. The humped image of Mr. Crowe labored near the edge of the ravine. He directed a flashlight at the outside wall of the inn. Was he checking the building for storm damage? Marcy strained to see, leaning out as far as she dared without being seen.

From out of the darkness a man appeared — *the same one she had seen snooping before.* The man's hardhat shone like a silver ball in the moonlight. As the two men met, angry voices floated up to Marcy's window. Without warning, the man jerked his arm back as if to hit Mr. Crowe. The old man raised his cane in the air in defense, but then he fell to the ground. The stranger's hat was a streak of light as he raced away along the edge of the ravine.

Terrified and shaking, Marcy scrambled to her brother's bed. "Phil, get up!" she shrieked. "Quick! Something's happened to Mr. Crowe."

Phil opened his eyes and turned over.

"Th-that man . . . he came back, and Mr. Crowe's hurt . . . down there."

"Huh?" Phil was sitting up now, and trying to make sense of what Marcy was saying. "You sure?"

"Of course I'm sure! Come on. Hurry! We can go down the fire escape." She decided not to wait for Phil but climbed out the window as she spoke.

Barefoot and in pajamas, they scampered down the rusty iron steps. Marcy led the way—until they stepped in the tall grass where she'd seen the old man go down. Then she fell back by Phil's side and pointed, shivering. Even from that distance, she could tell Mr. Crowe wasn't moving.

"Do you think he's dead, Phil?"

Phil opened his mouth to speak, but no words came.

When they reached the old man, Phil knelt beside him. The two of them stared down at Silas Crowe, now a crumpled heap on the rain-soaked ground.

"Is—is he still breathing?" Marcy's voice was no more than a whisper.

"Run get Dad, Marcy," Phil said. "I'll stay with him. And remember," he added, "keep your mouth shut about *you-know-what*."

Wasting no time, Marcy ran toward the entrance of the inn. Glad to see the light flooding from the windows of the sitting room in their apartment, she knew her father was still reading.

Within minutes Mr. Dunlap was kneeling beside the old man. Marcy and Phil were calm

now that their dad was there. Marcy rushed to fill her dad in on the episode with the stranger in the hardhat.

Mr. Dunlap checked Mr. Crowe's pulse and spoke softly to Marcy. "Go wake your mother. Tell her to call an ambulance."

After Mr. Crowe was on his way to the hospital and they were assured his condition was not critical, Mr. Dunlap called the police to report the prowler.

Eager to talk about the incident, Marcy told the officer how the man in the hardhat had threatened Mr. Crowe. She hadn't actually seen him hit the old man, she admitted, but she did see him run from the scene—which she knew always made a person look guilty. Phil listened in silence as his sister recounted the events she witnessed. Marcy knew he was listening to make sure she didn't tell too much. But she also guessed he felt bad because he had slept through it all.

The policeman pulled his car close to the ravine and shone a giant searchlight across the old inn and down into the ravine. Like a huge eye, the beam searched for the culprit.

The Fergusons had been aroused by the commotion and came outside to hear the startling news. Even though they hadn't liked Mr. Crowe very much, they hated to see anyone in trouble. Marcy and Phil had another cause for concern: who would take care of Mrs. Crowe while her husband was in the hospital? What would happen to her now?

Giving up the search for the night, the police left. After learning the prowler had not actually harmed Mr. Crowe but merely frightened him, the Fergusons and the Dunlaps returned to their apartments.

As Marcy and Phil were about to climb the stairs to their bedroom, Mr. Dunlap said, "Marcy, that old man actually owes his life to you. If he had stayed on that wet ground all night, he might have caught pneumonia."

Now is the time to tell him, while he's praising me, Marcy thought. She looked at Phil, but the scowl on his face let her know she'd better not give anything away yet.

The minute they reached their room, Marcy confronted her brother. "Listen here, Phil Dunlap, you're not as smart as you think you are!"

"No, you listen, stupid. We'll have to ask the old man first. Don't you see? It's *his* secret. We'll just have to slip her food until we can see him."

Marcy wanted to run to her mother and pour out the story. . . . But maybe Phil was right. Did they really have the right to tell?

She suddenly remembered the time she tried to hide a puppy she found because she was afraid it would be taken away. Maybe Mr. Crowe was afraid someone would take Mrs. Crowe away if they knew about her, or make the two of them move from the inn. That's why he was so mean, she decided—to keep people away.

But who was the prowler? What was he after? Did he know the old woman was there? All she really knew for certain was that this night was the longest of her life.

Dawn was breaking on the horizon when Marcy finally fell asleep.

13.
A Visit to
the Hospital

Marcy awoke with a start. The thunderstorm of last night had washed the earth clean, and this morning, diamond raindrops still hung on tree leaves.

Marcy began to worry even before she got out of bed. With Mr. Crowe in the hospital, she and Phil were responsible for sweet Mrs. Crowe.

In the kitchen, Phil had already put on a pot of hot water to make oatmeal for the old lady. The two prepared a tray and slipped down to see her.

They explained that Mr. Crowe was in the hospital, but she was not to worry because they would take care of her until he returned home. They were relieved when she appeared to be unconcerned. After her initial "Oh," her mouth becoming as round as her eyes, she slipped back into her happy dreamworld.

Back in their apartment, Phil and Marcy made plans to visit the hospital and talk with Mr. Crowe.

At lunch, Phil asked, "Dad, can you get us permission to see Mr. Crowe?"

Mr. Dunlap looked up, his eyes wide with surprise. "Well . . . that might be arranged."

"I don't think so, dear," Mrs. Dunlap said. "When I stopped by the hospital this morning, the nurse said he had been most uncooperative."

"I can imagine the time those nurses have had!" said Mr. Dunlap. Marcy knew her dad was remembering *their* first encounter with the old man.

"They're actually having trouble restraining him at times," Mrs. Dunlap continued. "Unless he's kept under sedation, he even tries to get out of bed. It seems he suffered a slight stroke that hinders his speech, and his ramblings make no sense at all. Do you really think it would be wise for the children to see him?"

Marcy felt certain she and Phil would understand his ramblings. "Please, Mom," she begged.

"It's an emergency," Phil added.

Dumbfounded, Mr. and Mrs. Dunlap looked at each other. "Well," Mrs. Dunlap said, "suppose we leave it up to the nurse on duty. All right, Tom?"

Within the hour Phil and Marcy were marching behind the nurse down a hall of the community hospital. Speaking over her shoulder, the nurse said, "I'm glad to learn the rumors I've heard about Mr. Crowe aren't true." Her voice was as crisp as her uniform, but Marcy thought she detected the trace of a smile.

"Wh-what rumors?" asked Phil.

"That children are afraid of him."

Marcy had felt nervous about coming to see Mr. Crowe, and now she became really tense. As far as she was concerned, the rumors *were* true.

"Here we are," the nurse said as she opened a door. Marcy and Phil followed.

The old man was alone in the room, lying motionless on the raised hospital bed, his ashen face almost as white as the sheet. His thick glasses lay on the bedside table.

Marcy had the impulse to run. He looks dead, she thought. Her panic-stricken flight from him outside the old section of the inn a few days earlier was fresh in her memory.

The nurse crossed to the bed and bent over

the corpse-like form. "Mr. Crowe," she said, "you have visitors." The old man grunted and the nurse motioned them over.

Marcy's feet would not move. "You go," she whispered to Phil.

"I'll be at the desk just outside if you need me." The nurse's soft-soled shoes took her away to other duties.

Marcy watched Phil edge up to the bed. Mr. Crowe had not moved and his eyes were still closed.

"M-Mr. Crowe?" Phil called softly.

Another grunt rose from the bed sheets.

"It's—it's me, Mr. Crowe—Philip Dunlap, the redheaded boy you chased."

The old man's face came alive. He opened his eyes and reached an arthritic hand toward the table, groping for his glasses.

"You—you don't need your glasses, sir. I—we—just wanted to tell you that we—Marcy and I—are taking care of her."

There was another grunt, louder this time as Mr. Crowe made an effort to lift himself up. His face looked pained as he tried again to speak. His gnarled hands clutched at the bars on the bed.

"She's all right, Mr. Crowe. We took her

breakfast." Phil rushed on. "But we can't go on keeping it a secret. We came to get your permission to tell Mom and Dad."

The expression of relief that flooded the old man's face was one Marcy knew she would never forget. Her courage now stronger, she stepped up beside Phil.

"She likes us," Marcy told Mr. Crowe, surprised at the calm in her own voice. "We've been playing with her."

The noise that came from the pathetic figure sounded like "yes, yes." They were sure of it when he closed his eyes and lowered his head once again on the pillow.

At first Marcy thought Mr. Crowe had fainted. Then, the creases in his face deepened into a smile and a tear rolled down his check. He gives the impression of being a hard, tough old man, Marcy thought, but he's really soft underneath, like a mother bird protecting her babies.

They tiptoed out, then rejoined their father in the lobby. On the way to the car neither of them could talk fast enough. Mr. Dunlap sat motionless behind the wheel of the car, the keys dangling in his hand, unable to believe all that had gone on without his knowledge.

Marcy and Phil weren't quite as eager to tell their mother. They knew they were in for a hearty scolding for trespassing. But they also knew there was no better person to look after Mrs. Crowe.

All the way back to the apartment Phil and Marcy interrupted each other as they finished the story for their dad. As they crossed the bridge to the inn, Marcy gasped. "It's the razing crew!"

Big work trucks were parked along the deserted side of the inn, and men in hardhats moved like ants over the dilapidated area.

Marcy jumped from the car, clasped her hand over her mouth, then shrieked, "That's him!"

"Marcy, whatever is the matter?" asked Mr. Dunlap.

"Which one?" Phil asked, bounding after Marcy.

"The one who's way out ahead of the others. The one shaped like a question mark," she shouted, running toward the work crew.

14.
Happy Ending

Marcy's shouts sounded an alarm. Alerted that he had been identified, the man ran into the woods behind the inn. With Phil's help, Marcy explained the situation to her dad and members of the work crew. Several workmen headed for the woods and quickly apprehended the suspect.

As it turned out, the man did not have a criminal record. Like Marcy and Phil, he decided Mr. Crowe was hiding something when he ordered the razing crew off the property. He was trying to get answers from the old man. Admitting he had gone about things the wrong way, he insisted he never intended to cause any harm.

The work crew foreman spoke with Mr. Dunlap. The unused section of the building was unsafe, he said, and *must* be cleared without further interference. The man was shocked to learn the reason Mr. Crowe had been so obstinate about keeping the workers away. He instructed his men to move to the far end of the building to begin dismantling.

Marcy sighed in relief. Her dad put his arms around her shoulders, giving her a squeeze, and assured her that arrangements would be made to move Mrs. Crowe.

Eager for Mr. Dunlap to see Mrs. Crowe's historical treasures, Phil led the way to the secret room. Marcy ran to the library to get her mom.

When Miss Pettus heard Marcy's news of Mrs. Crowe and her treasures, she forgot herself for a moment. Breaking the silence of the library, she exclaimed, "A trunk? May I come too?"

As the three crossed the bridge, Marcy skipped ahead, the complete story gushing from her as she moved.

"Marcy!" Mrs. Dunlap's voice stopped her daughter in her tracks. "An old elevator shaft? Basement? You might have been hurt. . . . You and Phil should never have trespassed!"

Marcy knew that was just the beginning of what she and Phil would hear, but right now she was too excited to think of discipline.

Miss Pettus's gait resembled a puppet worked by strings, as she tried to hurry without actually running.

When the three entered the secret room, Mrs. Crowe's little round eyes twinkled with delight.

"Why, this used to be a wine cellar!" Miss Pettus said, amused that the cubbyholes along the wall were filled with trinkets and bric-a-brac.

Mr. Dunlap and Phil were kneeling on the floor, bent over the trunk. Running his hands through his red hair, Mr. Dunlap opened his mouth several times to speak, only to close it again. After a few minutes, he let out a low whistle.

When he found his voice, he said, "I just can't believe it—an unrecorded duel and even the pistols used, money from the old Hamburg bank, and a journal by John Robert Pinckney. My, oh, my!"

Miss Pettus, standing beside Mr. Dunlap, looked as if she might faint.

Mrs. Dunlap was attending to Mrs. Crowe, talking to her in a gentle voice. Marcy heard her say something about a nursing home, and Mrs. Crowe responded with "Oh."

After a short while, Mrs. Crowe asked, "Can I sit in the sun?"

Mrs. Dunlap smiled. "Yes, you can sit in the

sun."

Mrs. Crowe appeared untroubled by it all. I guess Mom was right, Marcy thought, sometimes it is better if old people slip into a dreamworld. Mrs. Crowe seems happy.

As Marcy and Phil pieced together the whole story for their captive audience, Mrs. Crowe seemed to listen. Now and then she'd speak the name of someone they did not know — perhaps, Marcy thought, some guest from the inn's past.

"You know, we've got a real love story here for you romantics," Mr. Dunlap said. "A young woman fell madly in love with her riding instructor and married him in spite of her 'society' background. Evidently his love matched hers, for when she became old and senile he hid her away for fear he would have to give her up to an institution."

"Poor fellow," said Mrs. Dunlap. "He must not have understood senility at all but thought she'd gone insane and would have to be 'put away' if anyone found out. That just goes to show, we mustn't judge others in haste. After all, most people who act in peculiar ways have reasons for their behavior — often, reasons we don't understand."

Miss Pettus nodded her head in agreement. The little librarian still appeared to be in a state of shock. "Why, the value of the contents of that trunk alone," she said, "will take care of the two of them for a long, long time."

"You mean they'll sell them?" asked Marcy.

"Oh, by all means," Miss Pettus answered, "when they learn how the world craves such relics of the past. Yes, indeed, there'll be scads of bids from libraries and museums when they hear of these treasures."

Marcy could tell Miss Pettus was having a hard time containing herself. As for her dad, he was still rubbing his head and whistling.

After Mrs. Crowe was settled in the Dunlaps' apartment, Marcy, Phil, and their dad returned to the basement to pack some of the treasures for moving.

That evening the Dunlaps talked quietly in the sitting room until long after bedtime. With Mr. Crowe's permission, they had moved the trunk to their apartment where Mr. Dunlap could pore over the contents.

The entire conversation did not involve treasures from the past, however. As Marcy expected, she and Phil got a lecture for trespassing. Their parents couldn't feel too angry in view of the way things turned out—but *never again*, they said, did they want to hear of either of them ignoring the law in such a careless and dangerous way.

They don't have to worry about me, Marcy thought. She'd had enough of exploring old houses to last a lifetime.

Mr. Dunlap told his family how well his research had progressed—even before the discovery of the Crowes' trunk. They would be returning to New York soon, he said. In fact, they'd be home in time for Phil to get in some practice with the relay team and for Marcy to celebrate her birthday with Ellen.

Marcy thought she'd be happy the day she heard this announcement. But with everything that had happened, she wasn't sure. She had not wanted to come south and leave her friends, but she had such a good time in Aiken, she was not ready to leave. She looked at Phil. She knew he felt the same way.

The Dunlaps visited Mrs. Crowe in the nursing home where Mr. Crowe would soon be transferred from the hospital. Marcy, Phil, Sarah, and Jerry visited the hospital each afternoon. Marcy knew they proved the rumor false that children didn't like the old man—although she would never have believed it at the beginning of the summer. Mr. Crowe seemed pleased to see them, and the hospital staff said their daily visits helped more than the therapy he received to regain his speech.

After the local newspaper ran an article of the Crowes' historical relics and Miss Pettus told everyone the story of the beautiful romance that lasted all those decades, townspeople made extra efforts to be nice to the Crowes.

Just a week after Mr. Crowe's accident, the Dunlaps packed their station wagon and drove away from Telfair Inn. They took with them not only the fruits of Mr. Dunlap's research but many special memories.

Jerry and Sarah's parents promised them a trip to New York the following summer. And Marcy and Phil pledged to show their new friends *their* city.

As for seeing other Aiken friends again, Marcy had no doubt of it—after all, she had drunk water from Coker Spring!

Visit with Marcy and Phil again
in *The Mystery of Edisto Island*,
available at libraries, bookstores,
and directly from the publisher.

About the Author:

IDELLA BODIE was born in Ridge Spring, South Carolina. She received her bachelors degree from Columbia College and taught high school English and creative writing for more than thirty years, chiefly in Aiken, the city Marcy and Phil visit in this story.

Although the story and characters are imagined, the sites noted in *The Secret of Telfair Inn* are real. You can walk along the same streets where Marcy and Phil walked. You can visit old cemeteries and see where the town of Hamburg once stood. You can look down on the ravine's rail tracks where today freight trains run. You can escape the busy boulevards and stroll down side streets munching an ice cream cone under the shady canopy of old magnolia trees.

Telfair Inn was patterned after Willcox Inn, which is open to the public. Though there are no ghosts or hidden treasure in its basement, visitors are assured of having a good time.

Mrs. Bodie encourages you to visit Aiken, a beautiful city of horses and flowers and history. Follow the trail set by Marcy and Phil. Bring your parents—tell them it's fun *and* educational.

Other Books by Idella Bodie:
Carolina Girl: A Writer's Beginning
Ghost in the Capitol
Ghost Tales for Retelling
A Hunt for Life's Extras: The Story of
  Archibald Rutledge
The Mystery of Edisto Island
The Mystery of the Pirate's Treasure
South Carolina Women
Stranded!
Trouble at Star Fort
Whopper

HEROES AND HEROINES OF THE AMERICAN
REVOLUTION
(A Series of Biographies)
The Man Who Loved the Flag
The Secret Message
The Revolutionary Swamp Fox
The Fighting Gamecock
Spunky Revolutionary War Heroine
The Courageous Patriot
Quaker Commander

Sandlapper Publishing Co., Inc.
Orangeburg, South Carolina 29115
1-800-849-7263